Deep and Crisp and Even

PETER TURNBULL

Deep and Crisp and Even

St. Martin's Press
New York

Library of Congress Cataloging in Publication Data

Turnbull, Peter.
Deep and crisp and even.

I.   Title.
PR6070.U68D4   1982   823'.914   81-21459
ISBN 0-312-19092-1   AACR2

First published in Great Britain by William Collins Sons & Co. Ltd.

Deep and Crisp and Even

CHAPTER 1

It had begun to freeze at midday. The slush in the roads
set in solid troughs six inches deep and cars slid into each
other as brakes and steering became useless. Shivering
citizens sought refuge in cafés and bars and strangers
talked to each other, complaining in frosty breaths. It was
the kind of coldness that gets everywhere, creeping into
homes and workplaces, piercing joints and stabbing at
bronchial chests. At four in the afternoon the sky was
heavy and black and the buses slowly stopped as the diesel
fuel froze in the tanks and feed-pipes. The main roads
were gritted, but not the schemes: women in labour and
men with broken limbs had to be carried over the ice to
where the ambulance waited. People with frostbite sat in
the casualty departments. The cold wasn't carried on a
slicing wind: there was no wind. There was no shelter; all
you could do was to keep your hands in your gloves and
your gloves in your pockets, keep the heat turned up and
hang the bill, because this was one of those few periods in
late twentieth-century Britain when actual survival means
just that; survival with a capital S.

There seemed to be no respite from the cold, but at 11
p.m. the mercury forced its way up the thermometers in
the city. It was only a few millimetres of movement but it
was enough to make the difference between freezing air
and being warm enough to snow. The snow fell thickly
and settled without hesitation. PC Phil Hamilton glanced
at his watch when the snow began to fall, because snow
can capture an event in time and place and record it for
hours, sometimes days. That night the snow began falling
at 11.10 and stopped very suddenly at three the following
morning. Phil Hamilton committed the time to memory,

and he knew by the manner in which the snow had stopped falling that it marked the beginning of another freeze. The snow which had melted into cracks in the cement and masonry of the buildings froze and splintered the stone, making a sound like the crack of a .22 air rifle. Apart from his boots crunching the snow and the background crackle of his radio it was the only sound he could hear.

Buchanan Street marked the centre of Hamilton's patch and at the bottom he could turn either left or right. Right was Anderston Cross, the motorway, some old buildings, a lot of new buildings, two building sites. He went left. Left was Argyle Street pedestrian precinct. He began to walk down the north side and planned to walk to Glasgow Cross. Then it would be a secluded place for a quick fag, and after that back up Buchanan Street, by which time it would be nearly six, end of the shift, and home. He tried the door of each shop as he passed it. He liked working in the centre of the city because there was action and pace from ten to midnight, but after midnight the city calmed and the action moved to the schemes. The early morning in the schemes was the time for battles, stabbings, gouged eyes and broken heads. The time for breaking into houses, not through a window but a dozen guys knocking down the front door and smashing the place to hell. Phil Hamilton liked to work at the beginning of the shift and relax at the end. He liked it especially when it was ten degrees below freezing because then there wasn't much work at the beginning of the shift either. He felt he had the city to himself, and stopped at a shoe-shop window. He was looking for a pair of fur-lined boots because he couldn't feel his feet.

He first saw the man when he was two hundred yards away from him. The figure staggered from the shadows on the north side of the street and fell in the snow. Hamilton walked towards the man without altering his pace but without taking his eyes off him. The man didn't move and Hamilton decided he had a drunk on his hands, a drunk who had collapsed, a drunk who couldn't be reasoned with, who couldn't walk home. A 'drunk and incapable'. So far this had been an uneventful shift; the cold had kept most folk at home and the police had, by working together, been able to stop any battles from starting by keeping a high profile. By 3 a.m. he'd come to regard sleep by 7 a.m. as a dead cert. Now there was a black heap in the snow which meant sleep by eight if he was lucky.

At six he would report off duty and at 6.05 he would fill out the charge sheet. Under the Criminal Procedures (Scotland) Act, 1975, in the Sheriff Court of North Strathclyde at Glasgow the Complaint of the Procurator Fiscal against Black Heap in the Snow. The charge against you is that on the sixteenth of January in the forenoon in Argyle Street, Glasgow, being a public thoroughfare, while under the influence of alcohol you did conduct yourself in a disorderly manner. This being an offence of drunk and incapable.

If the heap in the snow proved to be argumentative Hamilton would lay the second charge; that on the same day and in the same place you did shout, bawl, curse and swear, and commit a breach of the peace. This being the offence of breach of the peace.

And if the man threw a punch Hamilton would lay the third charge; that on the same day and in the same place you did punch PC P246 Hamilton about his body all to his hurt and injury; this being the offence of assault. Hamilton didn't know what he was walking towards, but thought he had better start the procedure. He turned his head to the left and spoke into his radio and asked for the Land Rover to assist him. He was told he would have to wait.

The man was lying on his back and Hamilton knelt

beside him and, slipping his glove off, picked up the man's wrist. He couldn't feel any pulse. He wasn't surprised; his fingers were already numb; they were coarse at the best of times and curled more readily round a truncheon than they did round a limp wrist. Hamilton's wife was a nurse with long spindly fingers who had patiently tried to teach him to take a pulse, but he never could, he hadn't the sensitivity. He felt at the side of the man's head, he knew there was a pulse there, somewhere near the ear. But he couldn't feel a pulse at either side of the head. He slipped his hand inside the man's coat and felt something wet. He winced and withdrew his hand momentarily as he imagined his fingers sinking into the man's vomit. He couldn't feel a heartbeat and took his hand away from the coat and looked at it. He gripped his radio and said, 'Poppa Control from 246. Cancel the Land Rover. Ambulance to Argyle Street, urgent, man with stab wounds,' and heard the affirmative reply. He wiped the blood off with snow and slipped his numbed hand back inside his glove. He stood and looked about him. The snow lay in an even mantle, disturbed only by his footprints, and the reflected lights enabled him to see a long way. He could see the name over a shop at the far end of the street and even fancied that he could pick out individual bolts in the Central Station railway bridge and, turning the other way, he could make out the blue of the clock face at Glasgow Cross. It was very still and very quiet and the only people there were himself and the dead man.

An ambulance with snow chains drove along the street and turned in a wide circle and stopped next to the body. The crew nodded to Hamilton.

'Stab wounds?' said the driver.

'Looks it.' Hamilton took his note book from his breast-pocket. 'Can I take your name, Jim?'

'I'm McFadgen, he's McArthur. Unit 3.'

Hamilton scribbled in his book. McFadgen and Mc-Arthur lifted the man on to a stretcher and slid him into the ambulance. 'We're taking him to the Royal,' said McFadgen, swinging himself into the cab. It was just another body, all in a night's work. He didn't bother to switch on the blue flashing light as he drove away.

Hamilton watched the ambulance go. Fifteen minutes earlier Argyle Street had been smooth and white; now, with footprints, ruffled snow and deep tyre-tracks, it seemed to Hamilton that a virginity had been taken, and taken violently. There was even the blood left behind on the crumpled sheet.

Hamilton waited at the scene and couldn't think why he had grown to feel possessive about the snow. He was twenty-four, married, wanted to start a family, snow had ceased to hold a magic for him eighteen years ago, yet there was something about the snow that night. He'd seen it disturbed by things which had come to govern his life, footmarks, violence, blood, ambulances and bodies.

And later, when a second vehicle turned into Argyle Street, Hamilton added senior officers to the list.

Sussock stopped his car beside Hamilton, got out and said, 'Right, laddie.'

'Sir?'

'Well what have you got, laddie?'

'Not a lot, Sarge. One man, middle-aged, stab wounds, probably, came out of there.'

'I can see. Why haven't you been in?'

'No need. It's a blind alley, Sarge, only one way in or out. Looks like only one man's come out since the snow stopped, and he's in an ambulance.'

Sussock looked into the alley. It had no lighting as such, but the same play of lights on the snow which il-luminated the length of Argyle Street enabled Sussock to see twenty feet down it. He grunted.

Sussock and Hamilton walked into the alley. It was narrow and dark, staircases and turrets. A part of nineteenth-century Glasgow that is within a stone's throw, or a stagger, of multinational chain stores, gloom and damp lying within the spill of sodium lamps. They followed the man's last footprints until they stopped, or started, against a wall. He had staggered from side to side down the alley, probably clutching the walls for support, and, when there were no more walls to clutch, had fallen in the snow. Hamilton shone his torch around the alley; waste-bins and damp cardboard boxes. He shone the beam up the rusting staircases, carefully picking out the long-since bricked-up doors.

A vehicle drew up at the end of the alley. Sussock and Hamilton turned. It was a white Transit van with an orange stripe down the side and blue revolving light on the roof. Half a dozen police officers spilled from the back doors and trampled the snow. Hamilton flashed his light in their direction and scanned the waste-bins again. He didn't care about the snow any more, he no longer felt the city belonged to him. He was another uniform again.

Sergeant Rafferty approached Sussock and ignored Hamilton, who stepped backwards.

'Knifing,' said Sussock. He looked at the footprints which started against the wall and he looked at the stairs. 'Search it,' he said. 'Inch by inch, stair by stair, go through the rubbish and search the snow even if you have to shovel the stuff away and sift it.'

'What are we looking for?'

'I don't know. A knife would be helpful but I don't think you'll find one. Just search the alley and don't ask questions.'

Rafferty swung on his heels, presented his back to Hamilton and yelled, 'Right, lads!'

Sussock went back to his car because his ears were cold and there was a pain in his chest. Winter always was a pain in his chest. His wife was a pain, his son was a pain, being called from the sofa in the front room was a pain, and right then he couldn't use a murder. He told Hamilton to follow him.

They sat in the car and Sussock turned on the heater. 'Tell me,' he said. Hamilton told him and Sussock wrote some of it down.

Hamilton left the car and returned to his beat. He went to find somewhere quiet. He wanted to see some undisturbed snow.

Clues and evidence disappear from the scene of a crime at a rate which is directly proportional to the time between the commission and the discovery of the offence; and they continue to disappear after the discovery of the offence, and so detection is often a race against time. That is why half a dozen police officers crouched in an alley prodding the snow, and searched through rubbish; and it was why Janet Reynolds had her sleep disturbed. It wasn't the phone call that awoke her, it wasn't her husband's voice talking softly into the mouthpiece, nor was it the slight movement of the bed as he slipped from under the sheets. She heard water running in the bathroom and opened her eyes at the sound. She turned and found she was alone in the bed and saw her husband's pyjamas on the floor. She glanced at her watch; it was five minutes after 4 a.m. Outside it was quiet. She knew that her husband had risen as quietly as he could and so she turned and laid her head back on the pillow and pretended that she was asleep. Her husband came back into the bedroom and finished dressing, quickly and quietly, and went downstairs, switching off the light as he left the room. She heard him leave the house and start the car and listened as the sound of the motor died away. She switched on the dim light by the bed and pulled on her dressing-gown, and went downstairs to make some coffee. She was reading an historical romance: perhaps she could finish it before the children had to be up.

The body had been declared dead on arrival at Glasgow Royal Infirmary and it awaited Dr Reynolds in the mortuary in the basement of the building. It lay on a marble slab with a brick under the head and a label with a number on it tied round the big toe of the right foot. Also in the room was Detective-Sergeant Sussock and the mortuary attendant, a small man with glasses, who wore his hair plastered to his skull. There was a gleam in the attendant's eyes which Sussock found disquieting.

In fact, he found it very disquieting, and his eyes were drawn to the tall silver-haired pathologist as the only healthy thing in the room.

The room was cold.

'Well,' said Reynolds, peeling on his surgical gloves, 'We have a male, European extraction, apparent age about forty-five, height . . .' he stretched a tape measure, 'Five ten. Weight about twelve stones.' The mortuary attendant scribbled notes on a pad. 'Do you know who he is, Sergeant?' Sussock shook his head. 'No identification,' he said.

'Well, anyway,' Reynolds looked at the body, 'slight contusion to left forehead, abrasions to left cheek. Particles of grit in the abrasions. Very bad teeth, no apparent treatment for some years. Some very old fillings and one or two extractions, no there's no recent treatment and he was probably in some discomfort because of it. Dental records might be able to help your quest, Sergeant. Birthmark left lower leg. No other significant marks.

'Wounds to upper left chest, abdomen and upper abdomen in the area of the pancreas. Upper left chest, linear cut, five inches long, superficial, but would have bled a lot. Seems to have been caused by a downward stroke from the shoulder towards the centre of the chest, probably a failed attempt to stab at the heart. The two stab wounds in the lower body seem to have deep penetration.' Reynolds patted the man's stomach. 'Bloated, might be beer, but let's take a look anyway.' He smiled. Sussock found it a healthy smile, unlike the sinister look in the attendant's eyes. The tall lean man took a scalpel and drove a long incision from the top of the man's stomach to the bottom. Blood flooded onto the marble slab and spilled on to the floor. Sussock felt his own stomach convulse and his gorge began to rise; he looked at the ceiling and managed to keep the contents down. Neither Reynolds nor the mortuary attendant flinched. 'Bled internally,' announced Reynolds in a flat voice, and, thought Sussock, needlessly. Then he noticed the attendant scribbling and reproached himself.

'Time of death, sir?' asked Sussock.

'All in good time. You know it amuses me that there are almost an infinite number of places in the human body where you can stick a knife without doing a great deal of damage, yet the attackers always seem to know where the vulnerable points are, the shoulder, the neck, two lovely arteries there, the heart, or at the bottom of the rib-cage like our friend here. People who often have no knowledge of anatomy do a perfect job. It must be intuition.

'This man bled to death following three stab wounds, one to the chest and two in the general abdominal area. My guess is that the wound in the upper abdomen did the trick, the other two wouldn't have caused death if he could have been hospitalized soon enough. Time of death? Not long ago, about an hour.'

Sussock already knew the time of death; sixty-five minutes earlier PC Hamilton had seen the man fall in the snow; but Sussock wanted to say something, because he still wanted to retch, and he felt that by speaking he would somehow placate his stomach. The question came automatically, as part of the murder routine. What he really wanted to know was the time of the attack. He asked it then.

'It could have been anything up to an hour and a half before he died. Certainly it was after he bought a fish supper for his tea.'

'What about the attacker; are there any indications you can give about him, sir?'

'Or her, Sergeant. Well, it's hard to say. The lower wounds have a horizontal plane but the gash on the chest seems to have been delivered from above.' He made a downward movement of his right fist. 'That sort of way?'

'The attacker was a right-hander?'

'Probably, you can see for yourself that the chest wound is a cut stretching from the left shoulder to the centre of the chest, and it was cut in that direction, shoulder to chest, because the tissue is torn in a downward direction. The lower wounds were probably caused by a quick stab, like so,' he jerked his hands backwards and forwards at the level of his thigh.

'Did he put up a fight?'

'Let's have a look. No abrasions or contusions to the knuckles. He didn't hit his attacker. Plenty of grease and muck under the fingernails, which might contain something which would be of interest to you, Sergeant. We might as well take them off now.' He made an incision at each side of the finger- and thumbnails and then prised each one away with a pair of tweezers and dropped them into a glass jar. 'We'll send these to the lab, you'll get the results sometime this morning with a full post-mortem report.' He handed the nails to the attendant, who wrote a label and stuck it on the jar. 'The instrument which did the damage is a very thin piece of metal about eight inches long. Or, who knows in these days of advanced petrochemicals, it might be a piece of very hard plastic.'

'A stiletto, perhaps.'

'That sort of thing.'

Sussock knew the medical profession to be notoriously non-committal, and he had worked with Dr Reynolds before and knew that 'that sort of thing' was one of his most used phrases. Would you say that the hole in the man's head with burn marks round it was caused by a revolver being fired at very close range? Oh, that sort of thing. He also knew that Dr Reynolds would supply a very thorough post-mortem report, but at that moment he knew better than to press the pathologist for supposition.

It was 6.30 a.m. when Sussock left the mortuary and walked across the car park of the Glasgow Royal Infirmary to his car. It was still dark and the thin air hurt his chest. It made him think of his wife. He went back to P Division station and began typing his preliminary report.

Phil Hamilton was already at a typewriter, working furiously. He knew from experience to make his report as full as possible, to leave no question unanswered if he could answer it. It was as much for his sake as the force's, because he wanted bed and didn't want to be held back by questions. Davy Hamilton had worked as a welder with John Brown's; he wasn't an educated man but had a deep respect for wisdom and knowledge, and had taught his son a rhyme which was printed on a card he had found in a packet of tea. The rhyme was written by a man called Rudyard Kipling and ran:

'I keep six honest servingmen; they taught me all I knew.
Their names are what and why and when and how and
     where and who.'

The lesson had sunk in, and PC Hamilton wrote the six interrogatives at the front of each new notebook and used them in questioning, mentally ticking each one off as it was answered. He also used them in report-writing, which made his reports pedestrian, sometimes tedious, but always they were thorough. At the end of this morning's report he added a paragraph about the weather conditions, the time the snow started to fall and the time it stopped. He thought it might be important. He submitted the report to Sussock, who read it and told him to sign off. Hamilton was pleased, he'd be home earlier than he'd expected.

Sussock added Hamilton's report to his own, and, together with photographs of the alley and of the deceased, made up a file which he laid on the DI's desk. He went to the front desk and read the incident book for the night and then made himself a coffee. He sat in the canteen with his feet on the seat of the opposite chair, knowing somehow that this would be the last opportunity he would get for a rest for some time. Murders are like that. It was 7.30 a.m.

Detective-Inspector Donoghue came on duty at 8.30 a.m. The worst winter that the city had experienced for forty years didn't prevent him from being on time, and so no one else at the Division could avail themselves of that excuse. At 8.31 he was reading the file about the Argyle Street stabbing.

'What do you think?' he asked, closing the file.

'A mugging,' said Sussock, sitting in front of the grey steel Scottish Office issue desk. Donoghue wore expensive shirts, three-piece pinstripe suits with a gold hunter's chain slung across his waistcoat. He had a small moustache, an air of assured calm. He made Sussock feel uncomfortable.

'Why?' Donoghue reached for his pipe.

'No wallet,' said Sussock. He watched Donoghue flick his gold-plated lighter and knew that the DI would be surrounded by smoke for the next eight hours. 'He was stabbed for his wallet.'

'What about the money in the pockets?'

'Loose change.'

'Mmm. Who was he, Ray?'

'No idea.'

'What have you done to find out?'

'Nothing,' said Sussock. He hated prevarication both in himself and others. But, Christ, it was only a quarter to nine. Donoghue was silent, and Sussock felt three inches tall. 'I'll get on to it,' he said.

'Have the face made up for photographs in case no one reports a missing middle-aged male.'

Donoghue was referring to the process whereby a dead person's face can be made up with cosmetics, and the sunken eyes and cheeks artificially inflated, which has the effect of making the deceased appear more like a shop-window mannequin and less like a stiff. The result is close enough to the living and breathing version to have the photograph used on posters and for handouts at press conferences. Sussock thought that thinking of such things was the reason why Donoghue was a DI and he was still a sergeant. Sussock was older than Donoghue.

'Prepare a press release,' said Donoghue sucking and blowing on his pipe. 'Nothing special. "A man was stabbed to death in Argyle Street in the early hours of the morning. The man has not been identified. Police are appealing for witnesses." '

Sussock said he knew the formula. He also said the lab. reports and the post-mortem report would come in during the day.

'Fingerprints?' asked Donoghue.

'I'll get on to it.' Sussock winced inwardly.

'Anything else happen last night?'

'The rest was run of the mill. Five breaches of the peace, seven drunk and incapables, three assaults and one serious assault.'

'Quiet night,' said Donoghue. 'Dare say the cold kept most people at home.'

When Sussock had left his office Donoghue picked up the file and read it again. He didn't accept Sussock's theory that the attack was a mugging. The reasons why, he thought, were:

(1)   Very young people and very old people and very rich people are targets for muggers. Not middle-aged men who are tall and well built and do not appear to be particularly wealthy.

(2)   Mugging is out of character in Glasgow. It's a violent city but in 95% of the incidents of violence the victims and assailants are previously known to each other. Glaswegians use violence to settle disputes more readily than people in other cities. For a city of its size there are few acts of gratuitous violence. Your fourteen-year-old daughter is a lot safer in Glasgow then she would be in Liverpool or London. Whatever Glasgow women might think, they haven't got a serious rape problem, and Glasgow hasn't got a mugging problem.

(3)   If you are mugged you are threatened with violence, probably knocked to the ground; the violence used is that which is sufficient to make you relinquish your wallet, handbag, briefcase, carryout. You are not stabbed three times in the chest and stomach.

(4)   The muggings that do occur in Glasgow mostly take place in the schemes, and most victims are rumbled for their carryouts. They don't take place in the centre of the city, in the no-man's-land, where the lights are bright, where the mugger can't tell who's watching from where and can't tell who's round the next corner. Your mugger likes his own territory.

Donoghue put the file down at the corner of the desk. He didn't like it. Over the years he'd learned to listen to what he called his 'inner voice', and his 'inner voice' told him that this was something nasty, something to be wary of. He couldn't even hope that it was a gangland revenge killing; it was too messy. The only thing he did like about the file was Hamilton's report, and he arranged for it to be photocopied and distributed to the cadets.

By noon Sussock felt as though he had been on duty for a week. He'd arranged for the deceased's face to be treated and photographed and the result was a six-by-ten picture of a man whose eyes seemed to be staring in terror, but without the attendant facial expression; the lips were limp and the eyebrows low. But the photograph was good enough to use should the need arise. The fingerprints were taken and checked with the records held in the data banks of the National Police Computer. The N.P.C. identified the prints as belonging to one Patrick Duffy, aged forty-two, who had been paroled from Peterhead five years previously, after serving four years of a six-year stretch for robbery with violence. His discharge address was given as 278 The Hayes, Falkirk. Sussock telephoned the Central Region Social Work Department. They'd seen Duffy once, when he'd reported to his P.O. on the day of his release. 'You know how it is,' said the voice. 'Give us the staff, and we'll do the job.' So far as they knew he had no known relatives. 278 The Hayes was a lodging house. Sussock phoned Peterhead. They had no record of Duffy's relatives. His pre-admission address was given as 53 South Scott Street, Glasgow. Sussock didn't bother to write it down, he knew the address well—it was another lodging house. His one long-standing relationship seemed to be with a 'criminal accomplice', James Dolan. The voice from Peterhead said Dolan had died two years ago. Sussock checked the electoral register. Patrick Duffy hadn't registered to vote.

The lab. reports came in shortly after 1 p.m. Patrick Duffy's clothes were all old and of varying original quality, they came from a damp house and were infested. There were two pound notes and thirty-seven pence in change in his pockets. There was a cigarette packet containing three cigarettes and a half-smoked butt. He was wearing odd shoes. The report from the G.R.I. confirmed everything that Sussock had put in his report and added that the deceased had advanced cirrhosis. It also added that there were traces of blood of AB-negative type under the fingernails, there were also fibres of the material used for donkey jackets and duffle coats, and a human hair, light-coloured and from a male scalp. Sussock checked the front sheet of the report. Patrick Duffy's blood group was O, and his hair was black. Sussock typed up an account of his morning's work and handed it to Donoghue with the two lab. reports.

Donoghue read over the reports. They gave a tragic story of a wasted life, a lost life, what Donoghue privately referred to as a 'twilight existence'. But he was more upset by the implication in the reports. Patrick Duffy had money in his pockets, he had cigarettes but no matches. He was a derelict alcoholic. This was no mugging.

Donoghue sat back and pulled on his pipe. He saw a broken man shuffling down Argyle Street in the early hours of a snowy morning, shivering in damp second-hand clothes. He came upon somebody, a male, with light-coloured hair and wearing a donkey jacket or duffle coat who then proceeded to stab Patrick Duffy three times. It was a deliberate attempt to kill, with no obvious motive. Donoghue believed that motives for crimes against the person could be reduced to three: emotive, financial gain, and alcohol-related impulse. He couldn't see anyone being vengeful towards a pathetic figure like Patrick Duffy; there was no financial motive; and alcohol-related stabbings occur in or near the home when frenzied spouses reach for kitchen knives. He was then left with a chilling fourth possibility: the deranged mind, the criminally insane. The psychopath.

He suddenly went very cold.

Police Constable Phil Hamilton discovered the second body at approximately 1 a.m. on the seventeenth, twenty-two hours after seeing Patrick Duffy fall. The body was that of a young woman who had been stabbed twice, once in the stomach and once in the jugular artery. She was lying in the middle of a building site near Anderston Cross, a site which was obscured from view by billboards lining the pavements. Her eyes were wide, and stared up at Hamilton, who turned away and vomited on to the iced snow. He thought it just *had* to be him that found the body.

At 10 a.m. he walked out of the station and kicked at a mound of snow. He had just come out of Sussock's office, where he had been reprimanded for smoking on duty, because that was the only reason he would have gone on to the site.

Hamilton thought the city was a bitch.

CHAPTER 2

A psychopath grips a city in a certain kind of fear. It is a stomach-wrenching, heart-stopping fear. It is a fear which brings suspicion and distrust. It is a fear which causes strangers to look at each other with narrowing eyes. There comes a danger in walking alone, especially in darkness, because you are then victim to:

(a) the psychopath
(b) suspicion of being the psychopath.

Which of these two states is the least enviable is debatable. The consequence of one is óbvious. The consequence of the other is being cornered by a group of thugs holding tyre levers, hammers, swords, pick-axe handles and a 'this is going to hurt you more than it's going to hurt us' look in their eyes. It's little use arguing the toss with a group like this, especially if you're the third loner to lay the patter on them that evening, because they're cleaning the city, and there've got to be casualties when you clean a city. It is a fear which creates spurious assumptions; it's safe up to midnight, it's safe if you're a man/woman, it's safe unless the moon is full, it's safe if you have a dog. Girls who might otherwise risk the walk home rush for the last bus, lenient fathers become forbidding, knives, sprays, metal combs will be discreetly carried for self defence. This certain type of fear takes a stranglehold, because it's a fear of the unknown and it's difficult to remember that the reality behind the awful myth is one man with a knife, because this certain type of fear is called terror.

Donoghue stood at the window of his office and looked down on Charing Cross and the bottom end of Sauchiehall Street. He watched the people in the street, the men, the women, the office workers, the men in overalls, the drivers of the cars, the passengers on the buses. They were fathers and sons, mothers and daughters, they were happy and optimistic, they were dour and had problems to spare, they were wise and foolish, they were loaded and they owed plenty.

They were the people of the city.

Donoghue knew that he could send a panic like a demon from hell through a million people simply by turning and lifting the phone on his desk and arranging a press conference. 'Gentlemen,' he would announce, 'there is no connection between the two murdered people save to say that they were both killed by the same instrument in the same way and with no obvious motive.' Then a sharp hack with a taste for the sensational would interrupt and say, 'Does that mean a psychopath?' and Donoghue would say 'Yes, I'm afraid it does.' Some would rush for the door, others would stay for details, but either way the panic would start as the first editions hit the streets.

The dead girl was called Lynn McLeod. It was still only 11.15 on the 17th of January and there was still hope, a faint hope, that somehow Patrick Duffy and Lynn McLeod had a link in their lives, no matter how far back or remote, which could lead, no matter how tenuously, to a man with light-coloured hair who had killed them both for a motive, no matter how twisted. Donoghue hoped for anything which would mean that there wasn't a man with a pathologically warped psyche walking the streets of Glasgow, anything which would mean the two murders were two murders which would be added to the year's total and nothing more sinister. But deep inside he knew that it wouldn't be so, he knew that the ghost of Bible John was rising to stalk and haunt the city. Deep inside he knew it would get worse before it got better.

Already it had started. Behind him on his desk was the first edition of the *Evening Times*. It carried Patrick Duffy's photograph on the inside page and with the caption 'Do you know this man?' and then the telephone number of P Division police station if someone did. The write-up was an account of both murders, Patrick Duffy's and 'a twenty-year-old typist whose parents are being informed.' Her name and photograph would be in the later editions. The article finished with the sentence 'A police spokesman' (whom Donoghue knew to have been Frank Sussock) 'said' (as instructed) 'that the police are not able to say whether the two murders were linked'. It had been a response to a question put by a clever reporter who had printed the answer and left it up to the astute citizens of Glasgow to seize upon an implication that the police were very able to say that the murders were linked.

Also on his desk was the file on the murder of Lynn McLeod; she was in fact twenty-three and lived with her parents in Easterhouse. Her parents had been 'informed' in the middle of the night. Mrs McLeod had fainted and

Mr McLeod sat in his chair and stared at the wall. When the constable had revived Mrs McLeod he summoned a neighbour and drove back to the police station, stopping at the presbytery on the way. Later Mr McLeod would be asked to identify the body (but Donoghue knew that it would be a formality). There was no doubt about the girl's identity. Her handbag was lying next to her, and in the handbag was a transport card on which was a photograph of the face of the body which now lay wrapped in a white sheet, in a drawer, in a cold vault.

Donoghue found six interesting points to be drawn from the reports submitted by the G.R.I., Detective-Constable Richard King, and the luckless Hamilton.

(1) The time of death coincided approximately with the time of Patrick Duffy's death on the previous night.

(2) The cause of death was the same: stab wounds to two different parts of the body.

(3) The wounds of Lynn McLeod were caused by a long thin-bladed instrument.

(4) Lynn McLeod's purse, which was found inside the handbag, still contained nearly fifty pounds.

(5) There was no evidence of sexual interference.

(6) There was a human hair underneath one of her fingernails which matched that taken from underneath one of Patrick Duffy's fingernails.

W.P.C. Willems knocked and entered Donoghue's office and asked permission to take the reports for photocopying in preparation for the conference. Donoghue nodded.

He leaned back in his chair and clasped his hands behind his head. The murders were undoubtedly committed by the same person, a man who had light-coloured hair, had AB-negative blood and wore a donkey jacket or duffle coat.

He might be criminally deranged.

Donoghue rose and refilled his pipe. He pulled on his

overcoat and galoshes. The conference was at twelve. There was time to take a turn to the river and back. Clear air, clear mind.

P Division police station had been built in 1926. It had had continual usage since then, twenty-four hours a day, seven days a week, for over half a century, and it had a team of maintenance workers for whom there was always work. The drains blocked, then the heating failed, the wiring burnt out and the drains blocked again. All had to be repaired immediately because the building could never close. Over the years the personnel complement had increased and space had had to be found for sophisticated radio communication equipment and latterly a computer terminal. The result of this was to effectively make the building smaller, and successive Chief Superintendents had had to improvise: officers doubled up and shared rooms, files were stacked three-deep on shelves, and the cells were overcrowded. The only room which retained its original function was the armoury. Really little more than a small anteroom in the basement, it had a double-locked steel door behind which were six Lee Enfield .303 rifles, which dated from the Second World War, and two .38 Webley revolvers. There were also two locked boxes containing the ammunition, thirty rounds for the rifles and twelve rounds for the revolvers. A small room on the first floor with dusty windows had no designated purpose: it was used severally as an interview room, a holding room, a store room, a planning room, and that particular afternoon it became a conference room.

The conference started at twelve o'clock. Six people sat round the lightweight tables which had been 'liberated' from other rooms. Donoghue and Sussock sat on one side, Detective-Constables King and Montgomerie sat facing them, at the bottom of the table taking the minutes was WPC Willems. At the head of the table sat Chief

Superintendent Findlater. Chief Super Findlater was 'the chair'. In front of each officer was a file containing reports and all known facts about the stabbings of Patrick Duffy and Lynn McLeod. At 12.01 heads were bowed as the officers read over the reports. WPC Willems sat at the bottom of the table, notebook open and pen poised. At 12.10 only DC Montgomerie's head was still bowed and then he too looked up and sat back. Findlater cleared his throat. He was a baldheaded man who, even for a policeman, had an impressive bulk.

'Can we,' he said, in a rich Highland accent, 'formally convene the conference to discuss the murders of Patrick Duffy and Lynn McLeod on the night of 16th and 17th January respectively and which both took place in the vicinity of Argyle Street, Glasgow.'

WPC Willems put pen to paper.

'DC King has a verbal contribution to add to the report, sir,' said Donoghue.

'Yes, sir,' King sat forward and shuffled in his seat. He was twenty-five, bearded, had barely made the 5 ft 8 ins minimum height requirement and had never really lost his puppy fat. His voice wavered slightly as he spoke. 'I visited the home of Lynn McLeod this morning and took Mr McLeod to the mortuary to identify the deceased. He made a positive identification. I've only just returned so I haven't had time to write up the report.'

'All right, all right,' said Findlater.

'When I was at the house there were quite a few people there all milling round. By all accounts she was a rare lassie, no enemies, well liked.'

'They always are,' grunted Findlater, studying the table top.

'Universal opinion was that no one had any reason for doing her in. The priest was there and he reckoned she was the last person he thought would be murdered. She was a quiet lassie, took a drink but not much, didn't bother with the dancin'. She was studying Highers in the evening because she wanted to go to the University. She was mad keen to learn Russian, sort of obsessed with it. She had a boyfriend.'

'Oh!' Findlater stopped studying the table top. Donoghue took his pipe from his mouth.

'Yes sir, he wasn't at the house. They thought he was in England somewhere. They were quite close but her parents raised every objection in the book.'

'Colour of his hair?' asked Donoghue.

'Ginger.'

'Good,' said Findlater. 'We have a suspect. Mark that down for action please, Constable. Do you know where in England he is?'

'No, sir, but I have his home address.'

'All right, we'll come back to him. Is that all, King?'

'Not quite, sir,' said King apologetically. 'After her father had identified the body I brought him back to the station to pick up her things.' Findlater glanced at Donoghue.

'It's all right, sir,' Donoghue said calmly. 'We examined her possessions. They didn't yield anything.'

'That's not quite correct, sir,' said King. 'Mr McLeod went through the articles in her handbag; he was still in a state of shock, not checking that everything was there you see; he couldn't have known whether everything was there anyway . . .'

'Get to the point.' Donoghue was gripping the bowl of his pipe.

'Sir, in the handbag, crushed into a corner at the bottom, she had one of these bags that was more like a message bag, a canvas thing it was, still is; well, there was a small piece of paper crushed into the corner. There was blood on the paper and some writing.'

'Where is this paper now?' Findlater had leaned forward while King was talking and now eyed the young man coldly.

'At the lab., sir. I asked for the blood group to be identified and for any dabs, prints, to be lifted. I've asked for the results to be sent here, sir, even if it means interrupting the conference.'

'Good man. What was written on the paper?'

King took his notebook from his pocket and consulted it. He knew from memory what was on the screwed-up piece of paper the numbed father had pulled from the depths of his late daughter's handbag, but he also realized that a conference likes to see a stamp of authenticity and so flipped over the pages of his book. Then he said, ' "This is for Lissu." '

'Let me see.' Findlater extended a large, fleshy hand. King passed the notebook to Montgomerie, who passed it to Findlater. ' "This is for Lissu",' said 'the chair', more to himself than the conference. Findlater handed the notebook on to Donoghue and Sussock. It was then passed to Willems, who copied the spelling of 'Lissu'. King took the book back and pocketed it.

'Comments?' said Findlater.

'I take it that "Lissu" doesn't mean anything to anybody here?' asked Sussock. There was a shaking of heads.

'What does it mean?' said Sussock. ' "Lissu". Is it a movement, some organization, are these sectarian killings?'

'I hardly think so,' said Findlater.

'Is Lissu a person? Some kind of nickname?' Sussock appealed to the conference.

'Perhaps,' said Montgomerie leaning forward. 'We should start with what we know.' Donoghue grunted and lit his pipe.

'We believe the murders were committed by the same person. The method of attack, the weapon, and the hairs and the fingernails confirm that as near as damn.'

'They confirm it absolutely,' said Findlater.

'Very well. We know that the murderer had light-coloured hair and we know his blood group.'

'He *is* a male,' said Sussock, glancing quickly at Constable Willems.

'Do we know anything else?' asked Findlater. There was a silence, a looking at the table top, and a slow shaking of heads. 'So we are now left with the dangerous game of conjecture. Comments, please.'

'If we can establish a link between Duffy and the McLeod woman,' said King, 'that may help. We need to know more about both of them.'

Donoghue nodded.

'Any reaction from the press release?' asked Findlater.

'None,' said Sussock. 'It's a little early, though. I am also having a limited number of posters run up for distribution to libraries, bus and rail stations and the like.'

'There's the possibility that one was murdered for a reason, a premeditated murder, and the other as a decoy,' suggested Montgomerie. 'You know, to camouflage the intended murder.'

'It's a possibility,' said Sussock.

'It's a double-edged weapon.' Donoghue took his pipe from his mouth and knocked it gently on the ashtray. 'It can work just as effectively against the murderer as it can for him; twice the possibility of detection. I also think it's unlikely to be used by someone who chooses such a messy and dangerous—dangerous for himself—method of attacking his victim. Decoy murders are committed by people who don't like to get too near their victims; poisoners, shooters, people like that. Our man gets into a scrap with his victims.'

'Do we know why the McLeod woman was walking late in the city? It sounds a bit out of character for her.' Findlater looked at King.

'A drink after the office closed, sir,' said King. 'She phoned her parents' neighbours and said the girls were going for a bevvy to celebrate one of them getting hitched. She went along to be sociable. Had a couple of vodkas and went on to the grapefruit juice. When the bar closed they went back to one of the girls' flats for coffee and she was walking home back through town, either to get the 2 a.m. No. 41 to Easterhouse, or more likely get a taxi.'

'When did you find that out?'

'This morning, talking to the girls she went out with.'

'Very well. For someone to kill Lynn McLeod for any reason, as yet unknown, they would have to know when and by what route she would be walking back to the city centre. How many people could have known that?'

'None, sir,' said King. 'So far as I can tell. Only four girls went back for coffee and Lynn McLeod was the first to leave. She also took an unlikely route to the city centre. The flat they went to was just below the Mitchell Library. Most women and a lot of men would have stuck to the bright lights and turned right at Charing Cross and walked up Sauchiehall Street. She must have taken the earlier right turn and walked up by the Anderson Centre. It's a bit gloomy at night there, sir.'

'I think we can assume somebody chanced upon her,' said Findlater. 'I don't think she was deliberately ambushed. And that leaves us with Duffy. I can't see anybody wanting to do in a man who led such a life as he, no matter what he might have done in the past.'

'We don't have a motive,' said Montgomerie. 'That's what we are saying. There's no reason, so far as we can see, why Duffy was killed, and the two most common motives for attacks against women, sexual and financial, are not present in this case.'

Donoghue cleared his throat. He had a pipe-smoker's cough. It wasn't the deep, lung-shaking cough suffered by cigarette smokers, it was a shallow cough clearing an irritation at the back of the throat, and Donoghue used it to effect, this time to claim the floor; 'Good point, Mont-

gomerie,' he said. 'I think I want to echo that by sharing
my feelings about these murders, but I hasten to add that
I appreciate it is pure speculation. Montgomerie is right,
the lack of motive is significant. I don't think we can dis-
count the possibility that we have on our hands a person
who is killing for the sake of killing; someone who is
criminally deranged.'

Sussock said, 'God in Heaven' and Willems, who had
no right of access to the conference, groaned loudly. The
others sat in shocked silence.

'I appreciate,' said Donoghue, feeling he had to break
the silence, 'that it's too early to say yet, but in the
absence of other indications, I think it's the most likely
possibility.'

'As you say,' said Findlater, 'It's too early to tell. But I
am inclined to agree it's a possibility. Comments?' There
were none. The conference was still in shock.

'Very well,' said Findlater. 'Let's see what we have. Not
a lot, according to my notes. For action, investigate Lynn
McLeod's man-friend, and find out more about Patrick
Duffy, though after Inspector Donoghue's contribution I
think anything we find may be red herrings, but we can't
take chances.' He paused. 'We'll assume a routine murder
enquiry until we are forced to accept the Inspector's
theory. The Inspector will co-ordinate the enquiries.'

Donoghue said, 'Thank you, sir.'

'Sergeant Sussock and Detective-Constables King and
Montgomerie will be in support. I reserve the right to
assume command at any time and without notice.'

WPC Willems scribbled furiously.

'We'll need an incident room, Inspector.'

'I'll commandeer this very room, sir. I'll arrange for a
direct telephone line . . .'

There was a knock at the door. Willems glanced at
Findlater, who nodded. Willems rose and crossed the
floor to the door, opened it, and took the envelope which

was handed to her. Sussock watched her closely. Her hair
was done in a tight bun, she wore an unflattering black
dress which hung below her knees, dark tights and flat
shoes, and she still managed to look attractive. She handed
the envelope to Findlater, who tore it open and studied
the contents.

'It's the lab. report on the piece of paper found in the
McLeod woman's handbag,' he announced. 'No prints.
Bloodstain is AB-positive.' He glanced at the file in front
of him, 'It's the girl's blood. They photocopied the piece
of paper. You didn't say that "This is for Lissu" was
typewritten, King.'

'An oversight,' said King. 'I'm sorry.'

'That's an understatement if ever I heard one,' said
Findlater dryly. 'Oversight, you say. Didn't you see the
significance of this? It gives an indication of the coldness
with which this attack was planned. It virtually confirms
the Inspector's theory. Thoroughness, King, thoroughness in all things. Have a look at PC Hamilton's report.
That's the sort of reportage I want.'

King had his own opinion of Hamilton's reports;
juvenile, he thought, would be a kind description. 'Yes,
sir,' he said.

'Where were we?'

'Conclusions, sir,' said Donoghue. 'I'll arrange a telephone line to be installed, probably more than one in
fact, and it will be manned round the clock.'

'Good. At the moment Lynn McLeod's man-friend is
our No.1 suspect. Find him and bring him in for questioning. We'll assume the psychopath theory to be correct
in the event of a third body. Christ, I hope you are wrong,
Inspector; it will knock this city sideways. Try to find out
what "Lissu" means.'

'I have increased the foot patrols in the centre of the
city,' said Donoghue.

'Good. I'll take a verbal report from you at four thirty

each afternoon, Inspector. I hope to God you are wrong.'
     'So do I,' said Donoghue.
     Findlater rose, and the rest of the conference did
likewise. They left one by one, save for Sussock and WPC
Willems. Sussock smiled at her, then he too left the room,
leaving the tall girl to collect the files and write up the
minutes.

The murderer got into the lift. He was glad it was empty.
The steel doors closed, and he smiled at the womb-like
sanctity of the box as it carried him upwards. He left the
lift at the fourth floor and took the stairs to the seventh.
He pressed the button marked 'For Attention'. A young
woman with short hair, in a red dress, gave him a pro-
posal form and helped him complete it. She asked him to
take a seat, and walked away with the form.
     He noticed she had long fingers. Not stubby like his
own, but long, and they spread over the paper like a
bird's foot. In the corridor where he sat two men were
standing, talking. One said, the accident had happened a
year ago and this is them giving out the money only now.
The other man said, they are not so slow to take the money.
     The woman came back and sat next to him. She smelt
of scent, he thought it must be scent, he didn't know that
much about it, but whatever it was it was nice.
     'I've spoken to Mr Young,' she said in a whisper, 'and
he says it's necessary for you to have a medical before we
can approve the policy. We can arrange one for you.'
     The murderer stood and walked slowly towards the lift-
shaft, leaving the girl in the red dress sitting on the seat,
watching him go, and thinking what a lousy job she had.
He took the lift to the ground floor and walked on to the
pavement and became one of the crowd.

The man was dressed in slacks, slippers, and a vest with a
hole in the front. He held the door wide and surveyed

King suspiciously. King wondered if the man felt cold. If he did, he was showing no sign of it.

'It's about Tommy, y'say?' said the man. King nodded.

'You've identification?' King took his card out and showed it to the man. The man had an eagle tattooed on his left forearm, his hair was thinning and his stomach distended. He stepped aside and showed King into the living-room.

In the corner of the living-room was a bed; in the bed was a silver-haired woman with a pale, drawn face. The woman raised her head and glowered at King and let it sink back again on to the pillow. There was a chair in the room, and a table, on which was an ashtray full of stubs. On the wall was a photograph of soldiers in dress uniforms. In the fire grate two wooden chairlegs were burning, the small flames blistering the varnish but giving little heat. King suspected the couple had been subject to a warrant sale, All in Accordance with the Debtors (Scotland) Act, 1832.

"It's the police, hen,' said the man. 'About Tommy.'

'There's more trouble,' said the woman in a thin, cracked voice, and looked constantly at the ceiling.

'The wife's no' well,' said the man. 'Is Tommy in trouble again?'

'We don't know,' said King. 'We'd like to trace him.'

'Is it about Lynn?' said the woman from the bed.

'Yes,' replied King. 'We would like to talk to Tommy about Lynn.'

'You don't think he did it?' asked the man. There was a note of alarm in his voice. 'Tommy's been in trouble before, but that was years back.'

'Breach of the Peace and Assault. Four convictions,' said King, who had checked the records before driving out to Easterhouse. 'Last conviction was two years ago; he drew three months' Borstal training.'

'Aye, no bother since then, and not since he was going

with Lynn. He's calmed down and been looking for work.'

King said it wasn't easy, there was not a lot of work about. Then he shivered despite being dressed and in-doors, and he wondered again at the man's state of un-dress. He asked how long Tommy and Lynn had known each other.

'Eighteen months, they met the summer before last, she was a fine lassie, her parents didn't like Tommy, didn't think he was good enough, I suppose, but she went with him anyway. Strong-minded lassie, and the change in Tommy, he wouldn't do anything to harm her. I don't think he knows she's dead, he couldn't, we only just heard from them across the stairs. I wrote him a letter, I only posted it a few minutes ago, just before you came, sir.'

King hated being called 'sir' by working-class men who were old enough to be his father. 'He is a violent boy,' he said.

'Aye, he's a big lad, and he likes a fight. But not lately. Not since he met Lynn. He's on the way up, he'll be brand new when he gets settled. I don't know how he'll take it about Lynn. She was a fine lassie.'

'Where is he?'

'Corby. He's staying with my brother. He's looking for work and was to be sending for Lynn when he was fixed up.'

'They'd've been married,' said the woman from the bed. King thought the woman was dying. He didn't want to enquire after her health. 'How long has he been down there?'

'He took the bus just after Hogmanay.'

'He's not been back since?'

'No, sir.' King winced.

'We've got a card to say he'd arrived, but nothing since. Tommy never was a great letter-writer. Where's the card, hen, in the drawer isn't it?' The man left the room and returned a few seconds later holding a picture postcard of

Corby Town Centre. He handed the card to King. It was postmarked, 'Corby, January 5th' and Tommy Ferguson had written, 'Got here okay. Staying with Uncle David. Will look for work tomorrow. Love, Tommy.'

'Can I have your brother's address in Corby, please, Mr Ferguson?'

The man reeled off an address and King wrote it in his notebook. 'Do you know of anyone who was holding anything against Lynn McLeod?' asked King.

'No, no, sir. She was a fine lassie.' The woman in the bed croaked.

In the car King radioed in to P Division and asked that a request be sent to the Northamptonshire Police that Tommy Ferguson of 12a The Knoll, Corby, be brought in for questioning in connection with the murders of Lynn McLeod and Patrick Duffy. He started the car and drove back to the city via Royston because he wanted to avoid the congestion on the Edinburgh road. It was four o'clock and it was dark enough to need headlights. He drove through poorly gritted streets, narrowed with snow, past rows of crumbling council houses, and dim side-roads full of abandoned cars. Streets where he had sworn at policemen, attacked dogs with sticks and thrown rocks through windows. He saw two figures on the roof of Royston Baptist Chapel.

He slowed to a stop and reversed. The chapel was set back in the road and the two figures were kneeling on the roof tugging at the lead. King presumed it was the lead they were after. He couldn't see anyone tugging at the slates. He turned off the engine and switched off the headlights and radioed for discreet assistance. He left his car and walked to a 15-cwt van which had been parked at the gates of the chapel grounds. It began to rain, and visibility was almost nil. Inside the van was a collection of jemmies and lengths of rope. He took a match from his pocket and pressed it into the valve of the front off-side tyre. The valve hissed and a stench like rotten fish filled his nostrils. If the van belonged to the two guys on the roof then it was okay; if not, then kids did it, didn't they? He went back to his car and lit a cigarette.

A panda car pulled up behind him. The driver got out and sat next to King, who told him about the figures on the roof and the van with the jemmies and lengths of rope in the back. King offered the constable a cigarette; he declined and produced a pipe with a metal stem.

'Foul night,' said the constable. It was the extent of their conversation.

King watched the figures work their way across the roof. They worked methodically and efficiently, and half an hour after King had stopped his car the figures lowered a heavy canvas holdall to the ground and then slithered down a drainpipe. King and the panda car driver got out of the car and waited for the two figures to approach. They came out of the gloom and became two teenagers, walking towards the van. King turned and opened the boot of the car.

'Evening, lads,' he said. 'Just put it in here, please.' The two boys glanced at each other and then walked towards the car and dumped the holdall in the boot. The car's suspension sagged.

'Right, lads,' said King, shutting the boot lid. 'One of you with me, the other one with this gentleman.'

They drove in convoy to Royston police station and King left the charging to the constable. He drove back to P Division and walked into the incident room at 6 p.m.

Constable Shepherd was on duty. King nodded to him.

'Northamptonshire police already have Ferguson in custody, sir,' said Shepherd.

'Already! Why can't we respond like that?'

'No, I mean already, sir.' Shepherd blushed slightly. 'They already had him in custody when you called in.'

King took his coat off and slung it on a chair back.

Water dripped from it on to the floor. 'Why?' he asked.

'He assaulted a police sergeant, sir, pushed a broken beer-glass into his face during a pub brawl. They want to know if you still want to question him.'

'When did they take him into custody?'

Shepherd glanced at the notepad next to the telephones. 'On the fourteenth of this month, sir.'

'Ask them to ask him if he knows of anybody who would want to kill his girlfriend; other than that they're welcome to him.' King took his coat and walked through the station to his office. He would type out his report, then it would be a quiet bar for a quick drink, and I mean *a* quick drink, then home to Cathcart, his lovely wife and lovely children.

Then he thought about the letter that must be on its way to Mr and Mrs Ferguson of Easterhouse, and decided to extend his stay at the bar.

Ray Sussock got a negative response from the National Police Computer when he requested information about 'Lissu'. 'No data' read the printout, and that in itself held some significance, and he recorded it. His obligatory eight-hour duty had stretched to fifteen, there was no work coming in, nothing pressing for him to attend to, and he felt he had no choice but to sign out. He was paying a mortgage on a modest house in Rutherglen, and he drove there, leaving his car in the street, parked in the snow at the kerb.

'Oh, you're back,' said his wife. She was a small woman with a wrinkled face, who moved with quick jerky movements. She got up as soon as he entered the room and began to pace the floor with tiny, hurried steps. 'It's been fine all day without you, hasn't it, Samuel; now I suppose it'll be arguments, arguments, arguments.'

Sussock hadn't even taken his hat off yet.

'You are never here. When you are it's just fights. Anyway, you've missed your tea. We didn't know when you'd stop catching robbers so we ate it; anyway, Sammy was hungry. I dare say you can take yourself to the corner and get a fish supper. We won't mind, will we, Sammy?'

Sammy sat on the sofa. He was wearing tight black trousers and his legs were crossed. There was a ring in his left ear and he had taken the hair from his hands with his mother's lotion. He gave his father a transparent smile. 'We won't mind, Daddy.'

Sussock turned and left the house, pulling the door shut behind him. He heard the bolt being thrown across the door as he walked down the driveway towards his car. Wasn't it the male partner who determined the sex of the offspring? If he had run to a girl child would it then have been all right? Sussock drove to Langside because he didn't understand the world and needed solace.

The murderer's third victim saw her murderer before he saw her. She glanced at the man briefly and then lowered her head. The time was just before midnight on the seventeenth, the place was University Avenue, the visibility was poor, the thaw which had brought the drizzle was turning the snow into deep slush. The girl was walking up the hill, slipping in the slush, with her head bowed against the rain. The murderer slipped his right hand up the coat-sleeve of his left arm and gripped the wooden handle of the knife. He sat on a low wall and waited for the girl to reach him.

CHAPTER 3

Ray Sussock awoke in the small bedroom of a room-and-kitchen. The room-and-kitchen is as much a part of Glasgow as is John Brown's, the Railway Workshops, the River, and George Square itself. In the 1920s a popular type of tram was nicknamed 'a room-and-kitchen'. A room-and-kitchen is just that, one small room and one smaller kitchen, and an outside toilet shared with another family. A room-and-kitchen could be home for a family of ten, six room-and-kitchens to a stairway, sometimes nine to a stairway, each with a family. The Glaswegians used to live like mice in a haystack.

A room-and-kitchen had been Ray Sussock's introduction to the world, sharing a bed with his four brothers, pretending to be asleep while his mother and father bounced and snorted in the next bed. Stepping over the blood on the stairs and the vomit in the gutter. Lying awake one night listening to screams coming up the stairs, the screams which seemed to last all night, and the next day the stairway, the street, and the whole of the Gorbals learned that the woman had been murdered. Sussock rarely talked about the incident, but the screams had stayed with him and occasionally plagued him during a sleepless night. Sussock couldn't use any Gorbals nostalgia, he was glad to see them come down, and wouldn't walk where they had once stood unless he was compelled to.

The room-and-kitchen he awoke in on the morning of the 18th of January was the home of one person only. This seemed to make the room-and-kitchen just right; exactly the size needed for a single person living alone and with the occasional overnight guest. Sussock had known the owner of this room-and-kitchen (the scullery of which had been turned into a bathroom) for two years but had been sharing her bed only since the previous November. She was twenty-nine years old, a tall and shapely blonde with firm breasts, strong thighs and a flat stomach. She was lying next to Sussock, sleeping. The room was warm and comfortable, there was a chest of drawers in the corner, a bookcase, a deep carpet, a portable television in the corner and a Van Gogh print on the wall. Through a chink in the curtain he saw that there had been a fall of snow during the night. He rolled over and rested his hand across her thigh and nestled his head against her breasts. She stirred slightly. He felt his stomach protruding and resting against her and he wished he had not let himself go. Not for his sake, he didn't matter, but for her, the beautiful Norse goddess, who deserved better than him.

She had an alarm radio. At 5 a.m. it came to life; popular music, tinny and shallow, invaded the room, and Sussock wished it was 9 p.m. again, her smile, her arms around him, the intimacy, her understanding while they lay side by side, talking afterwards. He didn't want the day, he didn't want to be fifty-four years old, he didn't want a snow-covered city, he didn't want murders, he didn't want to be a plain-clothes policeman, a policeman in shabby plain clothes. He wanted her, her youth and beauty, he wanted the bed, just her and him.

She stirred and opened her eyes and smiled at him. He felt her eyes smiling too, and telling him to get up to dress, to go and do his duty. Sussock ran his hand over the stubble on his chin and felt unkempt. He managed a smile in return but knew his eyes betrayed his true feelings. She left the bed, naked, and walked across the room and switched on the electric heater. Another smile and she left the room and Sussock heard her washing in the cubicle. She returned to the bedroom and dressed. Sussock was itchy and sweaty in an empty bed. 'Up!' she said, no longer smiling. She left the room again and Sussock heard her in the kitchen, water gushing into the kettle and bread being sawn. He rose reluctantly and washed. Even a thorough wash and a close shave could only go some way to alleviate the feeling that he was second-hand, some way inferior. His legs were thin and his stomach touched the wash-basin as he leaned forward to shave.

In the kitchen a mug of tea and two slices of toast sat

waiting for him on the red Formica table-top. He sat and ate and sipped. He didn't speak because he knew that they were both waking up. She drained her mug and went back to the bedroom and moments later he followed. She was standing next to a stool in front of the dresser and held a hairbrush in her hand. She smiled again and Sussock sat on the stool and bowed his head and she began to run the brush across his scalp. When she had finished she bent forward and kissed his head, 'pretty boy', she said.

The woman finished dressing, black boots, black cape and white cap; and became WPC P137 Elka Willems. Sussock drove her into the city, dropping her near P Division station so that she could walk the last few hundred yards by herself.

'He struck again last night,' said Donoghue as Sussock entered the incident room. 'He's a nutter, no mistake, same method of attack, the lassie had only been in Britain for thirty-six hours. Left the same note; it was "for Lissu".' Sussock noticed that Donoghue had stubble on his chin and was bleary-eyed. He also noticed that the usually impeccably dressed Donoghue had trapped half his shirt collar under his tie. That couldn't happen to Sussock; like all policemen and prison officers who are likely to get into fights he wore a tie with an artificial knot which clipped over the top button of his shirt and which would come away in the hand of any thug who tried to garotte him.

'A lassie, you say?' said Sussock, feeling very uncomfortable.

'A German, came over the day before yesterday to visit her sister. The sister is under sedation at the Western Infirmary. They went on the town last night and got split up and the *Jungfrau*, hereinafter referred to as the deceased, was walking back to her sister's flat on Byres Road.'

'Any information?'

'She is nineteen. Was nineteen. Stab wounds to stomach and throat. Found by a motorist at 12.30 a.m., or thereabouts, she's being chopped up at the moment; the good Doctor Reynolds has had a busy time lately. Did you have a pleasant night, Ray?'

'I am sorry, sir.'

'They tell me they phoned your home and your wife didn't know where you were.'

'Yes, I . . .'

'So they had to call me, Ray. I'm a DI, Ray. My days of being called from my bed are over.'

'I'm sorry.'

'I live in Edinburgh, Ray, and the motorway is damn near blocked.'

'I know, sir.'

'I appreciate you have problems at home, Ray, and I'm sorry, but we need to know where we can reach you. Is there an alternative phone number you can let us have?'

'No, sir.'

'An address, then? So we can send a car for you.'

'I couldn't give it: it would compromise the other party.'

'Ray, you've reached retiring age but you've got enough in to opt for extended service. I know you are thinking about it. Whether you get it depends on current performance as well as record.'

'I understand.'

'Give it a thought, Ray.' Donoghue sat back in the swivel chair and relaxed his body tone. Sussock too felt himself relax, the inquisition seemed over. 'Anyway, now that we have a head-banger on our hands I've given instructions that I'm to be called first and immediately there's another stabbing. I will need you, though, Ray, so I'll probably drive round to Constable Willems's flat myself.'

'How did you know?'

'I didn't until just now.' Donoghue smiled. 'I'm surprised you fell for that, Ray. You shouldn't look at her so much and hang around after conferences when she happens to be the minute-taker.'

Ray Sussock was stone-faced. He didn't see the joke. In fact, he felt pretty stupid. It was Spot the Loony Time. 'I'd appreciate it if you'd keep it under your hat, sir. My missus is off her head and I don't think I'll be living with her much longer. I just can't, and my son just isn't my son, if you see what I mean?'

'I don't, but then in the kindest possible way I don't want to know. I appreciate that you don't want it broadcast about you and WPC Willems, but I don't make empty threats, Ray, and now I know where to get hold of you I shan't hesitate to come round and hammer on her door, and if I can't make it I'll send the nearest car. Buy her a telephone as a late Christmas present.'

'I'll come up with something, sir,' said Sussock, nodding. He thought it was one hell of a way to come to the end of an unchequered career and begin late middle age.

Press conferences are delicate operations. Donoghue had held them before, and, far from getting used to the ordeal, he found each one harder than the last. With each one there seemed to be the increased chance that this was the one where he'd blow the gaff, give away a vital piece of information about the commission of the crime which would lead to a spate of 'ghost' crimes and so cloud the central inquiry. Press conferences are as much about the withholding of information as they are about the giving. The policeman holding the press conference has to give what he intends to give and nothing more, he has to be on his toes continually. Newspaper reporters are not renowned for dim-wittedness and the police statement must be carefully checked, rechecked and rehearsed.

Donoghue was a frightened man. He was a firm
believer that men learn from their mistakes and as he had
never yet made a mistake at a press conference he felt that
he had yet to learn how to handle them. He sat at the
table in the rented room above the McLelland Galleries
in Sauchiehall Street, under the glare of the television arc
lamps, with Ray Sussock by his side and a tumbler of
water in front of him. He sat still, staring straight ahead
as reporters from the Scottish nationals and the local press
filed clumsily into the room and sat in the tubular steel
and canvas chairs which had been arranged in a line in
front of the table. Behind the chairs were the television
cameras and the recording technicians from the radio stations. Donoghue had shaved and had readjusted his tie
and wore a three-piece suit with his gold hunter's chain
looping across his waistcoat. His hands rested at either
side of the typescript he was to read out.

He felt so sick with fear that he wanted to leave the
room.

The reporters sitting in front of him were all men. One
or two were middle-aged but the majority seemed young.
A few had beards, neatly trimmed, and all looked to be
very fit on crime reporting. Donoghue was amused to see
that the reporter's traditional pad and paper seemed to
have been relegated to a subsidiary role in favour of portable cassette recorders which the reporters held on their
laps. They looked to Donoghue like a row of mothers
cradling their infants.

Control, he thought, must be the cornerstone of a successful press conference. Establish control at the beginning and half the battle is won. He raised his head slightly
and said, 'Thank you, Sergeant.' The door at the entrance to the room was shut, young men in army surplus
pullovers activated the cameras, tape recorders began to
spin.

'Gentlemen,' said Donoghue, fighting the urge to clear

his throat, 'I am going to read a prepared statement, copies of which will be made available at the table by the door at the end of the conference. I will answer questions at the end of the statement, but only if I think fit. If you should have a question, please indicate, and only ask once I have nodded in your direction.' He hoped it didn't sound as contrived as he felt it was.

'Gentlemen,' he said, focussing his eyes for the most part on a point just above the door at the back of the room, and only occasionally glancing down at the script, 'in the last three nights three people have been murdered, all in or near the centre of the city . . .' He went on to read a brief and censored account of the murders and summed up with the belief that the murderer was criminally deranged '. . . And what we know about the murderer is very little; he's male, probably wears a donkey jacket or duffle coat, has AB-negative blood, is probably right-handed and has light-coloured hair.

'It's vital that we trace this man before he can kill again. We appeal for anyone who knows of a man fitting this description or who saw anything suspicious in the early hours of the morning in central Glasgow on the nights of the sixteenth and seventeenth of this month, or in the West End on the night of the seventeenth, or early morning on the eighteenth, to come forward without delay. Any information will be treated in the strictest confidence.' He didn't think about the last sentence, it came automatically, as if from one of the dozen recording machines which whirred in front of him. Each reporter shot his hand towards the ceiling as Donoghue stopped talking. Left to right, he thought, and nodded to a young man with a beard and an expensive taste in sports jackets.

'Sir,' said the reporter, 'The murders are taking place with extraordinary rapidity; isn't that out of character for a psychopathic mind?'

Two of the reporters turned to each other and smiled,

thinking, probably, that it was a stupid question. Donoghue couldn't see the point of the question, unless the hack was questioning his ability as a policeman and accusing him of using the psychopath theory as an excuse for not doing any detective work. He was momentarily angered, but saw a way to capitalize on it.

'I don't know, is it? I'm not a medical man. We know that the same man has killed three people, leading completely separate lives, in the last three nights. If the pattern is continued he will kill again tonight. The significance of this is that there is more pressure on us all to catch this man than there would be if he was killing once every six months. Next man.'

'Sir, what advice can you give to people to ensure their own safety?'

That was more like it.

'First, never go anywhere alone if it can be helped. Try not to be out late at night, try to be in by midnight, report anything suspicious. Don't assume you're immune if you are a male, one of the victims was a male and he was also heavily built.'

'What about carrying weapons?' It was the same reporter. He shouted the question and Donoghue was worried that if he answered it then he would lose control and all would be shouting at him. However it was an important point so he took the question.

'Your best weapon is your own two feet, use them to run away and don't be afraid of doing so. If you get the chance, bring your knee or foot up into his balls, but don't hang around; this move is only to buy you time. Your second best weapon is your mouth, use it to yell and scream, it can frighten any attacker into flight, especially if he knows you're yelling for help and not screaming in terror. As for weapons, frankly I object to them because it's my experience that a lassie who carries a can of paint or a metal comb with a spike for a handle is only leaning on a false crutch. She gets to depend on it and when she's attacked she helps her attacker because she's standing there fumbling in her bag when she should be running and screaming. If a man carries a knife it's the same thing, it just encourages him to stand and fight. We'll have a hard job prosecuting somebody for carrying a metal comb or a spray can, but a knife, cosh, anything like that and we'll throw the book. There won't be any gun-law in Glasgow, head-banger or no head-banger. Next man.'

'Sir,' he was middle-aged; used a notebook in preference to a recorder. 'Will you be making use of the services offered by Scotland Yard?'

'No. Next man.'

'Sir,' youngish, no beard. 'Can you say something about the method of attack? Were the victims mutilated in any way?'

This was the question Donoghue had been afraid of. If he refused to comment it would strongly imply that there was a degree of mutilation which would be upsetting for the relatives of the victims, and which, when the truth was exposed, would harm the credibility of the police. But if he told the truth he ran the risk of telling all the lonely people in Scotland who can't make anybody listen to them that the quickest way of getting a lot of attention is to go out and stick a knife in someone without the need to hang around for any grisly business. There was really only one thing he could say.

"No, I can't. Next.'

'Sir, were the victims killed by a single knowledgeable penetration or multiple stab wounds?'

This was much the same sort of question, and Donoghue began to feel that he was wriggling on a hook. The reporters wanted answers, and were not letting him away easily. Once, during a police conference, this issue was discussed and an alarmingly senior police officer had suggested that a way of tracing psychopathic killers was to publish details of the attacks, thus encouraging 'ghost' crimes and so flushing out the psychopath by forcing anonymity on him. Donoghue had said that he found the suggestion professionally distasteful and ethically indefensible. Two months later he won early promotion.

'I can't answer that in case it encourages similar crimes,' he said with finality. 'Next.'

'Is there any significance that you have been able to discover about the word "Lissu"?'

'No. As you know notes reading "This is for Lissu" were found on two of the three bodies. Certainly it means something and probably holds the key to the entire case.' He paused. 'Frankly, we are baffled. "Lissu" may be a political movement, a religious cult, a person, anything. We would be grateful for any help the press can give us about "Lissu". It's a tantalizing clue. Next, please.'

'Can you tell us something about your background and police career, sir?'

'Next man.'

The *Evening Times* alerted Glasgow to the monster in its midst and the radio and television news hammered the message home. That night the city was quieter than usual. Those who did venture out followed Donoghue's advice, which was faithfully relayed by the media, and went about in groups or in pairs. There was a strong police presence. The murderer broke his pattern and did not strike that night, or was given no opportunity to do so. The next morning the dailies carried the story as a leader and two republished Patrick Duffy's photograph, but the telephone number had been changed and the papers printed the numbers of the direct lines to the incident room. All the papers tried to dub the murderer, 'the knifeman', 'the midnight murderer', 'the Glasgow stabber', but he wasn't finally named until a few days later.

The press conference brought a strong reaction from

the public, mostly anonymous, and all informing of men with light-coloured hair who wore donkey jackets or duffle coats. All had to be followed up.

It was a dark stairwell. Midnight black inside. There was light on the bottom of the stairs, it came in through the close mouth, there was light at the top landing, it came in through the skylight, but the middle of the stair was pitch black. Six doors, six names; it took Montgomerie six matches to check the names on the doors. The stairway was cold, on each landing were wooden chests, old and full of coal, and there was the extra door; the shared toilet. Montgomerie still found this aspect of Glasgow difficult to cope with. Bearsden was nice to grow up in, Edinburgh Law School was cool, he had drunk coffee in darkened rooms and talked about the meaning of life, he had had strange half-explored relationships, had sat in rooms with weird music in the background and sweet-smelling tobacco in the air. Life was the issue of getting into Zen, or getting into TM; it was the girl who disturbed his meditation to announce she was getting heavily into candles, the flame, man. She wore a red poncho and once did a drawing of herself and her man screwing in the bath. A third-class degree and Montgomerie returned to Glasgow, he put on a uniform and went on to the streets. He found life was a heap of crap. The sixth match flickered in the dark and Montgomerie saw the name 'Cameron' on a fancy tartan background. He rang the doorbell.

'Mr Cameron?' said Montgomerie when a man opened the heavy black door.

'Aye?' said the man.

Montgomerie flashed his I.D. card.

'Aye?'

'Can I come in?' asked Montgomerie. 'I've a few questions.'

'No,' said the man.

'We're making routine enquiries, Mr Cameron. I understand you wear a donkey jacket?'

'Aye, and I've got light-coloured hair, as you can see. I read the papers.'

'Can you tell me where you were on the nights of the sixteenth and seventeenth?' Montgomerie already had a feeling that he was on a hiding to nothing with Cameron.

'Aye, but I'll no'.'

'Just tell me and we won't bother you again. Otherwise I'll lift you now on suspicion.'

'O.K.' said the man, 'I was working.'

'Working?'

'Working.'

'Where?'

'Somewhere between Coatbridge and Newcastle.'

'Doing what?'

'Why?'

'Just answer the question, Mr Cameron. The sooner you answer the questions the sooner I leave.'

'All right. I'm a rail guard. This last week I've drawn the night shift. I was working when those people got knifed, running container trains to Newcastle for the Geordies to take on to Peterborough, then the East Anglians run them on to Harwich. We pick up a train in Newcastle for the return journey. One trip out and one back is an eight-hour shift. Ask anyone.'

'I will,' said Montgomerie. 'Coatbridge depot, is it?'

'Aye. Was it that cow down the stair that sent you here?'

'Can't say. It was an anonymous tip-off. I wouldn't tell you, anyway.'

'Sorry you've had a wasted journey,' said the man, coldly.

'We won't know it's wasted until we check with your ganger at Coatbridge. Do you want to make life easy for us and give us your work number?'

'No.' The man shut the door, plunging Montgomerie into the gloom.

King sat in the cell, leaning back against the chair with one foot on the table. A fair-haired young man with a round girlish face and a pert, turned-up nose sat on the other side of the table. He was looking at the floor.

'Let's have it again,' said King.

The man shook his head. King sighed and took a packet of cigarettes from his jacket. 'Smoke?' he asked. The man nodded and took a cigarette and held it between shaking fingers while King lit it.

'Again,' said King.

'I've told you once.'

'The head man round here, he's a particular man, Jamie, he likes to be certain.'

'I've told you the truth.'

'Tell me again. Apart from the head man being particular I've got a bad memory and I didn't write it down the first time.'

'You can't keep me here, not without charging me.'

'Who's keeping you, Jamie, you can go any time you like, you're helping the police with their inquiries, Jamie, just like a public-spirited citizen should.'

'O.K., I'll go.'

'Sit!' snapped King. 'There's no hurry, the bars will still be open when you do get out. Nice head of hair you have, Jamie, long and blond, always been like that, has it?'

'I'm no' queer.'

'I didn't say that you were.'

'You meant it.'

'Why are you so touchy, Jamie?'

'I'm not touchy.'

'What were you doing out last night?'

'Walkin'.'

'All by yourself, a cold night for walkin', Jamie?'

'I was warm.'

'Aye, donkey jackets are warm.'

'Aye, so they are.'

'So why walk by the riverside at two in the morning, in the cold and the snow?'

'Why not?'

'Why did you run from the officers?'

'I thought they were three guys jumping me. I told you.'

'You thought they were three officers going to arrest you.'

'They came at me from three different directions, running at me.'

'Didn't you see their nice shiny buttons, Jamie?'

'I just took off.'

'You knew they were polis, Jamie, and you were shit-scared. You still are. I'll make a deal, Jamie, clean break from you and I'll put in a word on your behalf.'

He shook his head.

'Why did you do it, Jamie, how many was it, three? Why?'

'I don't know, I . . . I didn't do nothing.'

'What don't you know, Jamie?' King sat forward, taking his leg from the table.

'I . . . I, why I'm here, that's what I don't know.'

'You said you didn't know why you did it. Of course you know, tell me, Jamie, you get these feelings, right?'

He shook his head, tears rolled down his face, over soft cheeks which had never needed a razor. The cigarette smouldered between two trembling fingers.

'Tell me.'

'No.'

'Do you get a kick out of it, Jamie?'

He shook his head again.

'I think you must.'

'Maybe I do.'

'What do you get a kick out of?'

'Nothing! I don't get a kick out of nothing!'

'That's why you did them in, for kicks.'

'It wasn't. I didn't do nobody in.'

'Yes you did. You did three.'

'No!'

'Where do you stay?'

'Partick. You've got my sheet, you know I stay in Partick. Glassel Road, Partick.'

'Just testing, keeping you on your toes. Stay alone, do you?'

'You know fine well I don't, Mr King. There's my dad and my wee sister.'

'Some son, eh?'

'I pay my way.'

'With what do you pay your way?'

'Social Security money, mostly.'

'Mostly?'

'I get some from horses and dogs.'

'What do you do when you don't sleep at night?'

'Walk.'

'What for?'

'Because I don't sleep.'

'Why don't you sleep good, Jamie?'

'I don't know.'

'Conscience troubling you, is it?'

'No.'

'Jamie, you walk at night, just you and your blond hair, all wrapped up not as snug as a bug in a donkey jacket, in the coldest winter this city's seen for forty years and you tell me you do it for nothing. Come on!'

'Leave my hair out of it.'

'What were you doing out?'

'There's a law against walking?'

'With your record we'll find a law against you walking, especially at two in the morning.'

'I've done nothing!'

'Want to go back inside, Jamie?'

He shook his head.

'Didn't have a good time, did you? Nancy-boy bug-gered in the cells.'

'I'm no' queer.'

'We could get a reduced sentence, fix you up with a psychiatrist. We'll arrange special facilities.'

'I done nothing, Mr King. I don't know what you're talking about.'

'What did you do with the knife, Jamie? Went in the river, did it?'

His head sagged forward, he held it in his hands, and breathed deeply. When he raised his head there was a broad grin across his face.

'You think I murdered those people? I didn't, see? I was in Paisley nick when the first one was done. They picked me up for being in a battle in a bar.' He sat back in the chair and pulled on the cigarette. 'Check,' he said.

King checked. Jamie McPherson had been detained in Paisley police station at 10.30 p.m. on the sixteenth. He had appeared before the Sheriff the following morning and was ordained for reports, having been charged with Breach of the Peace. King hadn't a clue what Jamie McPherson had been up to, but he certainly wasn't the man who had stabbed three people to death. King released him.

Thousands of men who wore donkey jackets or duffle coats, who had light-coloured hair and who lived in the Greater Glasgow region were not having a good time.

Sussock stepped into the living-room. It had a pungent smell. There were old fish-supper cartons piled in the fireplace. Half a dozen empty Carlsberg Special cans stood on the table and three more full cans rested on the arm of one of the chairs. The woman swayed from side to side, but managed to shut the door.

'Good night last night, was it?' asked Sussock.

'I don't remember much about last night, big man. This is my breakfast. You want a can?' She leaned forward and took a can from the chair arm and levered the ring-pull off with a plastic bangle which hung around her wrist. Hard Mary. 'See me, big man, I'm lawful, that's why I phoned when I saw Pat's picture in the paper. Pat lives in the top flat. Pat lived in the top flat. I own that flat and this one, big man, my man left both to me, left them both the two of them, in his will, to me. I'm his widow. I stay in this one because the roof leaks so I put Pat up there. Pat came from Tyrone and said he never had a chance. The Environmental, the Environment, the Health people say the roof's got to be repaired.'

'Can I see his room?' asked Sussock.

'Take a lager, big man. I don't get a lot of company, not since my man died, I don't know when it was, I can't really remember, but it doesn't matter, does it, do you think I'm attractive, men do, did, no, do.'

'The room,' said Sussock. 'Just let me have the key, hen.'

'How old do you think I am? I'm pretty.' She twisted slightly to let Sussock take in her profile. 'My husband used to tell me I'm pretty. I think I'm fifty-five, I bet I look thirty, I mean, not many women of my age can wear jeans and a T-shirt. How old are you, big man? I think you are forty, let me see, a bit more, yes a little bit more. Anyway, let's have a drink to eternal youth, or the snow. Or we could drink to Pat. Poor Pat. I need a tenant for the flat upstairs since Pat won't be back. I'll take anybody so long as they pay. Do you know of anybody?'

'Just give me the key, will you?'

'There was only one. Pat had it.'

'Shit!' said Sussock.

'Don't know why he carried it, lock's been bust for

years. Come and take a drink to the old times when you
come back, it's warm in here,' said the woman as Sussock
left the room.

Patrick Duffy's flat was as empty as his life. One bed
with a rug for a top blanket, a blackened toilet, Page
Three girls stuck on nails which protruded from the wall,
or trapped under paintings and a mirror. There was a
D.H.S.S. signing card in the drawer of his dresser and a
few old and dirty clothes. Sussock left the room in order
to breathe. He felt it had been a wasted journey, he didn't
want to do it in the first place but Donoghue had said he
had to go, the woman had called in and her call had to be
followed up for the sake of completion if nothing else. For
the sake of completion Sussock pulled the door shut
behind him and went down the stair and didn't call in at
the lady in the bottom flat for a drink to eternal youth, or
to the old days, or to poor Pat Duffy from Tyrone who
never had a chance.

He stepped out of the close mouth and into the snow.
He looked for a place to buy some coffee.

See me, I'm going to knock this city on its ass. I read
that in a book. I read a lot. One man says to the other
I'm going to knock this city on its ass. Ass is American
for arse. I like it better so I'm going to knock this city
on its ass. See me, I'm going to learn them, all of these,
they're going wrong. I like to read a lot, I read in
libraries and I like to know what went wrong before
and how all these buildings came to be here so I read
up history and I met Lissu. They've gone wrong so I've
got to learn them. I didn't know I had to till Lissu told
me. He tells me when to go and learn more. See, I'd
like to learn the welfare lady, the new one, but Lissu
hasn't told me yet. I read a lot.

CHAPTER 4

Thursday, January 21st.

Five days into the enquiry. The incident room was overrun with files, stacked on the floor in alphabetical order, cups of cold half-drunk coffee accumulated on the desk, the team had begun to develop an *esprit de corps*, bleary eyes and stubble on chins were taken as signs of industry and commitment, familiarity began to creep into professional relationships.

They had found out nothing.

By the morning of January the 21st P Division had logged one hundred and thirty interviews and had eliminated one hundred and thirty suspects. There were no other suspects. The enquiry had already cost thousands of pounds, other investigations had been dropped, and the information obtained was precisely nothing, zilch, flat round zero. By the 21st of January Inspector Donoghue had no more information than he had had a few hours after Patrick Duffy had fallen in the snow. The mood in the station was depressed, too many heads were sore from being banged against the brick wall.

Familiarity began to creep out of the professional relationships.

In the corridor just outside the incident room Ray Sussock in his top-coat and hat, and Elka Willems in a neatly pressed white shirt and a pile of files in her arms, stopped to talk.

'When do you get off?' asked Elka softly. Walls have ears. In police stations the walls have a lot of ears.

'Ask me another.' Sussock turned a hand palm upwards. 'I'm away up to Maryhill for a drink in a bar with a guy. I'll be back at five.'

'That's all you've got to do is it, old Sussock? Drink in bars when there's a bampot with a knife out there?'

'I wish it was. This is not just any guy.'

'All right, all right. Listen, I thought you'd take me for a meal tonight. If you can't get off I'll understand.'

'Pick you up at eight.'

'Fine.'

Elka Willems mouthed, 'I love you' and Sussock reached out and squeezed her arm. Then they walked briskly away from each other.

The bar was called the Auld Hoose and was on Maryhill Road. The Auld Hoose was in fact quite a new hoose, a bar in the classic Glaswegian style, a purpose-built drinking factory. It was a squat and a square building, battleship-grey pebbledash, one very solid door and no windows. It stood isolated on a site full of rubble from demolished houses. There was snow on the rubble. It was the sort of building which makes Englishmen who are used to pubs reel with culture shock.

Inside, the bar was dimly lit by soft red lights fixed to the walls, the gantry ran the length of the wall, the seats were wooden benches set in cubicles. The carpet had a red tartan pattern and was still damp from the previous night's alcohol. Sussock felt his feet sink into the carpet as he walked across the room. At the gantry he bought two double hits of Bells and a bottle of American Dry. He carried them over to where Sam Alphonso was sitting in the corner cubicle underneath the colour television set. He was a small man with a sallow pock-marked complexion.

'Eh, Raymond,' said Alphonso as Sussock approached.

Sussock put the drinks on the table and they shook hands. 'You want Sammy's nose and ears, I think.'

'Could be, Sammy,' Sussock sat down. 'Could be I'm jiggered and want a quiet drink. I thought I'd find you here. How's things?'

'Che sera, sera.'

'How's the book trade?'

'I make a bit. You still provide the main source of income, Raymond.'

'Money's tight at the moment, Sammy, we pay only for good news.'

'Okay.' He took his whisky.

'You've still got to keep scratching my back.'

'I knew you didn't want my company, Raymond.'

'Some other time we'll have a drink. Right now I need help.'

Sussock had known Alphonso for ten years. Shortly after he'd arrived from Turin he got into bother. Sussock put a word in for him and the sheriff admonished him. New man in town, said Sussock, had too much *vino*. Sussock had introduced Alphonso to the leaders of the Italian community and over the next ten years Alphonso had made a living by ingratiating himself into the fringes of the underworld, and by selling the harder-core glossy mags. He took a single end in Maryhill and sent for his wife. He readily took money for the information he passed to Sussock but Sussock always had the impression that the motive was partly an act of obligation to the man who had set him on his feet in this bitch city, and a Catholic act of contrition for trading in pornography.

'You want information about the head-banger?' He finished his drink.

'Right first time, Sammy. How did you guess?'

'I haven't seen you in six months, then this happens in your patch, then I see you. I reckon they must be connected. It's the way I reckon that makes me a good grass. I just point in this direction and say, "that way, but no guarantee".'

' 'Nother? Bells, all right?'

'For me it is the same.'

Sussock went to the gantry and bought the drinks.

'I don't know if I can help you, Raymond,' said

Alphonso as Sussock sat down. 'See, I've heard nothing, I don't expect to hear nothing. I've read it in the paper. See, these guys, Raymond, they're not human, they are wolves, how do you call it, scaly, scaly monsters slithering in the shadows, they don't plan, they don't have contacts and they don't have a loose mouth. Such men are not men, Ray, I'm going to hear nothing.'

'Listen to what we know.'

'I know what you know, Raymond, you know this yin's a male, he's fair-haired, and wears a duffle coat. Just like mine, maybe I dye my hair blond and go out in my duffle coat and stick someone. You want to run me in, Raymond?'

'You got an alibi?'

'Sure I've got an alibi, if I hadn't I'd fix one.'

'Just ask around for us, will you, Sam? Any strange characters, use the numbers in the paper—that's a direct line into the incident room.'

'I'll talk only to you, Raymond.'

'O.K., I'll likely be there. I'll tell you something the papers don't know; he uses a stiletto.'

'I'd say that's your best tack, my flat-footed *compadre*. Not a lot of stilettos about, it's an assassin's knife. In Sardinia they use them so well that they leave a little trace on the skin, a little mark, unless there's close inspection it looks like death from heart failure because all the blood goes inside.'

'I know,' said Sussock. 'I saw the P.M. on the first victim.'

'Was there a lot of blood outside?'

'A bit, on the chest there was quite a lot.'

'How many times were they stabbed?'

'Two twice, one three times, all in the stomach, the two women had their throats punctured and the man had his chest cut. Keep that under your hat.'

'Amateur.'

'That right?'

Sammy Alphonso nodded. 'See, Ray, a pro would only use a stiletto once. I think this yin's got hold of a knife and he's having a go at anybody. It's just chance that he's got hold of a stiletto.'

'That doesn't help a lot.'

'It helps plenty. It means you can rule out people who've been in the Commandos and the SAS because they'll know how to do it right. All this yin knows about knives is what he's picked up from that,' he jerked his thumb towards the television.

'Point taken,' said Sussock.

'It's the stiletto that's the big lead, Raymond. Difficult to get hold of, you want a Chieftain tank? O.K.; a stiletto takes a little longer. But, for you, I'll ask some questions.'

In the incident room, Donoghue, King, Montgomerie and the duty constable stood around the table. On the table was a cassette recorder and two polythene bags. In one bag was a letter and the other bag contained an envelope.

'Play it over again, please,' said Donoghue.

The duty constable leaned forward and rewound the tape. He pressed the 'play' button and stood back. The tape was of poor quality and there was a lot of hiss. They listened intently to the voice.

'So it's Fabian, is it? Detective-Inspector Fabian Donoghue. Some game we have, eh, Fab? I can call you Fab, can I?' (Low drone in the background.) 'This is Slow Tom, the midnight knifeman, Fab, just letting you know I know you're chasing me, but will you get to me in time? I did three in three nights, I'm having a wee rest, then I'll do in some more, I liked the girls best, the way they folded, and it's all for Lissu. Do you like girls, Fab? I wrote you a song, Fab, this is how it goes:'

(Flurry of guitar playing)
'I kill, kill, for Lissu, fast as I can.'
(Twelve-bar blues guitar playing)
'I go stab, stab, yeah, one, two, three
They all fall down, I said, one two, three.'
(Twelve-bar blues guitar playing)
'What's my favourite number?
Well, I like nine, yeah, nine is fine.'
(Twelve-bar blues guitar playing)
'Well I got three, fell in the snow,
That's six fat humans yet to go.'

There was a silence. The four policemen watched the spools slowly turning, and then the voice said:

'Well that's it, Fabian, Fab, I'm sorry, not *Top of the Pops* material, but it'll keep you on your toes.' (Low drone in the background.) There was a pause. 'Listen, Fab, I might pop something in the post again, give me a few days, but here's a clue to stop you getting too cold; you've got my hair all wrong — it's black.'
(Laughter)

The tape ran silently to the end. The other side was blank.

'So now we know what he sounds like,' said King. 'I didn't imagine him sounding anything like that.'

'How did you imagine him sounding?' asked Donoghue.

'Sort of a high-pitched, squeaky voice.'

'I thought he'd have a deep, slow voice,' said Montgomerie.

'What about what he says about his hair?' Donoghue looked at the two DCs.

'I don't buy it,' said King. 'We've taken three separate samples of male hair from three victims, each matches the others, and they're all light-coloured.'

'I agree,' said Donoghue. 'He's trying to throw us off the scent. Let's listen to what he didn't want to tell us.'

'Sort of mellow voice,' said King. 'Middle-class, but not quite.'

'Not at all,' said Montgomerie.

'More middle than working.'

Montgomerie didn't argue further.

'We'll get a voice expert to settle the argument,' said Donoghue. 'Interesting background noises. Comments, please?'

'Two aeroplanes flew over in the space of this tape,' said Montgomerie. 'I timed them, a minute between each, he's under the flight path of an airport, maybe out by Abbotsinch.'

'Perhaps,' said Donoghue. He tapped his pipe stem on his teeth. 'Interesting that that was the only noise which got into the room?'

'So he's living in a secluded spot,' said King. 'A remote house near the airport?'

'Or an old building,' said Donoghue reaching for his battered leather tobacco pouch. 'Come on, gentlemen, I don't want to do all the work. What about the acoustics, you can hear them best when he's doing his instrumental bit.' He rewound the tape, hitting and missing until he came upon a spread of guitar playing. 'Big room, don't you think? The tape has a hollow and an echoey sound.'

'It's a Spanish guitar,' said King.

'Acoustic as opposed to electrical is all our untrained ears can offer in the way of opinion. Think! We have a guitar-playing male who's softly spoken, he's in a large room under the flight path of an airport, and he has some hi-fi equipment. He can spell, too.' Donoghue indicated the note which lay in a cellophane bag. It said:

EARTHBOUND

Fab, I couldn't want for a more worthy opponent.
Here's a gift, or is it a gauntlet? Whatever it is, consider
it the first in a series.

Slow Tom

'He posted it in Glasgow yesterday, we'll send the letter
and envelope off to the forensic lab, but for the moment
what can they tell us?'

'He lives in the city somewhere,' said King. 'If he posted
it from near his home.'

'A student type?' suggested Montgomerie. 'Living in
rented rooms in the West End, right under the flight path
of Glasgow Airport. If he stays in the gardens off Byres
Road and in one of the top rooms his tape machine
wouldn't pick up a car backfiring unless it was right
underneath his window.'

Donoghue beamed at him.

Montgomerie was to look back on the 'Glasgow Knife
Murders' with a great deal of nostalgia. The case involved
teamwork, it had depth, it had crisis and pressure, it
came to have a great deal of fame, with the predictable
professional spin-offs for those who had been involved;
for a period after the case, to say he had worked with
Donoghue enabled a career-conscious policeman to virtually write his own references. One of the lesser spin-offs
for Montgomerie was that it gave him the chance to live
in his favourite habitat; a university campus, and to wear
his favourite plumage; faded denims and a beard.

The tape, the letter, and the envelope were sent to the
Forensic Science Laboratory, Scottish Office (Glasgow)
by courier. In the covering letter Donoghue requested
that they be given urgent attention. They were given very
urgent attention and were returned to Donoghue with a
full report later the same day.

The report on the tape told him little. The cassette was

three or four years old and had been wiped clear of fingerprints. A voice print was taken and was enclosed with the report. No two voices are the same, and each will leave its own trace on a voice recording machine, the printout of which looks like a seismograph recording of an earthquake and which will record the same characteristic modulations whether the owner is reciting Shakespeare or screaming at Hampden Stadium. They have the same drawback as fingerprints; one isn't a lot of good unless you can match it up with another. The report on the letter and envelope read:

JK/CT   Forensic Science Laboratory
                               Glasgow

Inspector F. Donoghue   21 January
Strathclyde Police
P Division.
G.3.

REPORT OF FINDINGS OF INSPECTION
OF LETTER AND ENVELOPE SUBMITTED 21.1

Envelope A4 brown manilla. Postmark genuine. Saliva under stamp indicates male person with blood group O. No trace of lipstick or scent on envelope seal or stamp. Therefore no indication of feminine involvement.

Letter Lined white vellum. Single sheet. No apparent smell. Sample placed in metal box and put on top of radiator to 'encourage' smell. Test result negative.

Writing made by black ballpoint pen. Sample held at fine angle to light. Indentations left on paper by previous letter visible. Fine pencil run over paper revealed letters, 'hol' or 'bol' or 'tol' at top right of page. 'Working hard' at mid

page. 'Love to' at bottom of page. I hope this
information is of use to you.

J. Kay, B.Sc., Ph.D.,
Dept. of Forensic Science.

'That blood group is some fly in the ointment,' said
Donoghue, holding the report in his left hand and a cup
of coffee in his right.

'It's a bloody great spanner in the works,' replied
Sussock, whose head was still light following his lunchtime
drink with Sammy Alphonso.

'But it tells us something, Ray. It tells us our man is
clever enough to know that blood group can be determined
from a saliva sample.'

'Or he's just lucky that somebody was willing to stick
the stamp on for him, probably before the envelope was
addressed.'

'We'll only know that when we catch the bugger,' said
Donoghue. 'We're getting to know something more about
him; he's intelligent, he's socially integrated, see, he's
sending love to someone, and at the top of the page here,
"hol", "bol", or "tol", that must be part of an address.'

'He's giving a lot away. Can't be deliberate.'

'I don't know. I'm beginning to see him now, Ray, I'm
beginning to get into his mind. He's enjoying the game
he's playing, it's called "catch me if you can". We've got
to grab him before he kills nine people, and he's already
got three. I reckon he'll stop at nine and call it a won
game, unless he likes being centre stage, in which case he
won't stop until he's caught.'

'He's clouding his trail,' said Sussock. 'He doesn't in-
tend to get caught.'

'I don't think so.' Donoghue hooked his thumb over his
pipe and watched a white car negotiate Charing Cross
and put itself at the morass that was Sauchiehall Street.
He reached behind himself and picked up his lighter from

his desk top. 'See, he's laying false trails, not clouding the one trail. He thinks he's clever, if he's a university student he probably thinks he's cleverer than he actually is, I know I did, and he probably thinks he's cleverer than the police, so he's laying a series of false clues, like contra-dictory blood groups, signposts to dead ends to see if we can sort out the relevant from the irrelevant.' He lit his pipe, pulling and blowing. 'Ordinarily it would cause us no great trouble because we'd follow each pointer until we were certain that it was a dead end. Do you follow?'

'Yes, sir,' said Sussock.

'But he's put a time pressure on us, he's knocking them down like flies and he's after six more. He's forcing us to take chances and guess. I bet he's the sort of smug, arro-gant bastard you meet from time to time that makes you want to chuck him in the river. Picture him, Ray.'

'Dangerous game, sir.'

'Won't go beyond these four walls.'

'Young, blond, a bit smooth, has the sort of smile that could sell toothpaste.'

'Do you think so? He hasn't got a beard, I just can't see him with a beard, beards don't go with arrogance, not often, anyway. You're right about him being young, slim as well, I'd say, he's a quick mover, he's got to be on the slim side. Carries himself with a sort of cocky swagger.'

'And his eyes are too close together,' said Sussock.

Donoghue laughed. 'Arrange a press conference, Ray, an hour's time, no need for me to be there, just a question of distributing copies of the tape to the radio and tele-vision stations and photocopies of the letter and envelope to the press. Someone may recognize the voice or the handwriting. Wonder why he didn't type it? Anyway, prepare a press release, inquiries continuing, concen-trating on young adults, suspect believed to be a student, possibly staying in the West End. Mug something up, Ray.'

Sussock mugged something up and nervously took the press conference. The reporters tried to force a question and answer session, but Sussock stuck to his guns. 'Just look on it as one big press release, boys,' he said. The conference was in time to make the later editions of the *Evening Times*, which led with the headline:

' "Slow Tom" — Glasgow Knifeman named.'

The restaurant was quiet; soft music in the background, only one other couple and they were at the far end of the room. The waiters leaned in a corner talking to each other, cloths draped over their shoulders. One waiter had huge hands and used them when talking, gesticulating wildly. The man dropped his credit card on top of a piece of paper which one of the waiters had laid discreetly at his side. The man felt very heavy and clumsy and awkward, but then he had expected the woman to say what she had said.

'I'm sorry, Ray,' she said quietly, breaking the silence. 'I do love you, but you have to understand, I don't even think you are ready for divorce. You seem to think it's your fault that your wife's off her head and your son came back from London a screaming queen.'

'Don't say that.'

'I'm sorry, Ray, but that's reality. It can't possibly be your fault. Stop punishing yourself.' She reached across the table and took his hand.

'I'll have to leave her, Elka,' he said, using his free hand to pour the remaining Chianti into her glass, 'But you're right, I can't make the break, I'd like her to do it.'

'But she won't. You're exactly where she wants you, captive in marriage.' She raised her glass, 'Here's to your future health and happiness, great Sussock.'

'I just can't exist in her presence. I get a pain across the front of my head and I feel that everything I do is wrong.

I feel big and old and gawky.'

'But you're not big and old and gawky. I should know.'

'If you'd marry me it would make the break easier.'

'Only because you'd be moving from one comfy middle-aged existence to another. If you were determined to leave your wife you'd do it whether I was here or not. Does she know about us?'

'No,' he shook his head. 'She hasn't been out of the house for years, she's like an animal pacing in a cage. The only thing she cares about is what happens under her roof.'

'You see, I'm not influencing anything at home. It would be just the same if you spent the evenings alone drinking coffee in a late-night grill instead of taking me for a meal and to bed.' The other couple had stopped talking to each other and sat in silence. They were leaning back in their chairs and staring at the table top. It seemed a relationship in death-throes.

'I love you,' said Sussock, suddenly.

'And I love you,' replied Elka Willems. 'But I won't marry you. I won't marry anybody. I've told you before and I don't want to tell you again. The people of my generation have a problem, I think; see, our parents, they fought a long and a hard war and after it there was a peace and a brave new world, free health care and education for all. My father was in the Dutch resistance and they put him in Treblinka. He survived and came to Scotland, he had suffered for this peace and wanted a part of it and so he had a family. But since then nothing's changed, I know what education system my children will have, I know what stages my marriage will go through, because I saw the marriage of Pieter and Flora Willems. There's nothing new I can give to my children, no new world, nothing, they're even going to eat the same sweets that I ate, Mars Bars and Bounty Bars. There's nothing original I can do by getting married. Ray, I'm twenty-nine, big two-nine, I hit the sound barrier later this year, but my horizons are still wide, if I get married they'll come rushing in and I'll know what's going to happen next because I've seen it, like I said. I'm being original and creative by being single.'

'Marriage is creative, Elka.'

'I think that's starry-eyed naivety. And you of all people should know better.'

'One bad marriage doesn't mean every marriage is not going to work.'

'Maybe we'd better break it off. The message just isn't sinking in, is it? You're not the first man to show me the altar doused in moonbeams, and you probably won't be the last, but the answer's going to remain the same.'

'I need you.'

'Look, Ray.' She pulled her hand away from his and held both hands up before her face. 'Can you see, Ray? I don't even wear decorative rings, I love you, but I love my freedom more. You have to accept that; it's a real part of my existence. It's a love me, love my freedom situation that you're in.'

'Point taken,' said Sussock, feeling stupid.

'Don't bring the subject up again, Ray, don't even think about it or I'll make the decision for you.'

'All right,' he nodded. 'Contract signed and sealed. Contract is that there is no contract.'

'That's better,' she smiled warmly. 'Tell me, have you decided about extending your service?'

'I've already applied,' Sussock returned her smile, 'But, like Fabian says, a lot will depend on current perform-ance as well as record, so if I play a big part in netting the head-banger I'm in with a big chance.'

'Good. I like men who are confident of themselves.' She reached out for his hand. 'I think you can make it, I've faith in you, old Sussock. Why don't you call a taxi and we'll go home and celebrate your new lease of life?'

It was Thursday night in Glasgow. The snow lay in three-foot drifts, the roads were slush, people walked in groups. Two drunks, swaying and falling, staggered down Hanover Street, one tried to land a punch on the other but couldn't swing, the other held him up, they fell into a bus queue, people stepped back, the drunks went on, swearing. They were in their early thirties, wore open-necked shirts and denims as though it was the height of summer. Two constables saw them and called up the Land-Rover. The drunks were arrested.

Two cars were driving through the city, one going east and the other going south, both motoring with a capital M, throwing up the spray like speedboats. They met at Renfield and Bath. Chests into steering columns, one passenger was wearing a seat belt and caught a whiplash on her neck; she wouldn't walk again. The other passenger wasn't wearing a belt and went through the windscreen. It could have been the road conditions; it may have been that both drivers were drunk. The police would piece the accident together, but only one driver would be liable to prosecution. The other was dead.

A father went into the city mortuary on Brunswick Street, and stood while an attendant peeled back a white cloth; the man said 'yes' and began to weep. Under the sheet was his daughter, she had been found in the Forth and Clyde canal when the thaw melted the ice.

A woman came into P Division station; she was wringing her hands and she said that her little boy hadn't come home. The desk constable took his pen and said, 'Name, please, Madam.'

Men came out of the Curzon Cinema where they had been watching 'Naked Exorcism' and melted into the night. In Langside two people were loving. In Bearsden a company director threw his baby girl against a wall because her crying prevented him writing his report. In a bar in Queen's Park a man with a lot of empty glasses in front of him sat back and began to sing 'Flower of Scotland.' In another bar a group of men huddled and growled about what they'd do to the head-banger, this 'Slow Tom', they'd tied him to a car and kick him to hell. He wouldn't make it to hospital.

It was a Thursday night in Glasgow, and Malcolm Montgomerie sat in the Rubáiyát. He was making an attempt on his personal record; he was about to try to slice it in half. His personal record for the time it took to get from first meeting to action in the sheets stood at four hours, ten minutes, and he reckoned that with this lovely child in blue-jeans he could make it in two, two and a half at the outside.

He'd hung around the university buildings and student cafés, he'd bought some second-hand law textbooks to enhance his image, and he had a specially obtained student identification card which was folding authentically in his hip pocket. The whole place was just alive with yellow-haired students carrying acoustic guitars. He called in at the university folk club, where only one performer had light-coloured hair. He sang without accompaniment, he had a girl-friend who lifted his beer to his lips and another friend who went with him to the toilet. All this because his hands were small and permanently clenched and stuck out from his shoulders. After he had sung he got a table-thumping, boot-stamping applause.

Montgomerie went upstairs to the television room; he was looking for someone from the West of Scotland, and saw only Commonwealth students reading the *Economist*. He was looking for males, and saw only university females in tight blue-jeans. Montgomerie was six-foot-plus, he had broad shoulders and a stomach he could lay a ruler across; he now had a trendy beard and loped along in casual, effortless strides. He had a coolness he turned on for the upper-set ladies, he had the man-of-the-world calm assuredness for the girls and he could roll his eyes for the older woman. In the television room he forgot the man with light-coloured hair and began to look at the tight jeans.

He bought a coffee from the machine and carried it to where the girl was sitting at the end of a low table. She was wearing Doc Martins, Levis and a fisherman's smock. Montgomerie saw her eyes widen as he sat down, and he knew that he was on to a winner.

Her name was Gillian Corr and she was reading biochemistry, though before Montgomerie's gambit she had been reading the *Beano*. He told her he had left the police force to take a postgraduate diploma in law. He hoped to teach in a university, he said. Gillian became very interested and put the comic aside. In the Rubáiyát he bought her drinks and allowed her to buy him a round. She told him about her parents, how they always fought, and he listened as though he was really terribly interested. Gillian invited him back for coffee and Montgomerie, glancing at his watch, said that that would be very nice, yes, perhaps a quick one. As they walked through the slush and the rain, he slipped his arm around her waist, spreading his fingers to make his palm feel larger. In bed she was all arms and legs, clutching him like her own, her very own bumper-sized teddy bear. Montgomerie slipped his watch from his wrist and put it on the floor, glancing at its face as he did so. Two hours thirty-six minutes. Not bad, Charlie Brown, not bad at all.

Gillian gasped, sharply.

See, I could learn her, or her, but they're with somebody. I haven't seen one alone the night. They walk in groups or with men. There was one standing alone but she was in the bright lights. Lissu says I have to learn an old one, not the Welfare bitch, he hasn't told me yet, but he will. That will be my reward. There's a lot of Filth on the streets the night, the way

they look at you, just wanting you to give them a reason
to turn their little blue light on. It's cold, the slush is
beginning to freeze, it'll snow again the night. I'm going into the back streets before the Filth get suspicious.
I did some reading last night. I read a lot.

CHAPTER 5

Elka Willems nudged Sussock. He stirred and in his sleep
said something unintelligible. She nudged him again,
driving her elbow into his ribs. He turned over and she
kicked his shin with her heel, encouraging his waking process sufficiently to allow the sound of hammering to
penetrate his sleep. He dreamed briefly of railway wagons
moving across a bridge, with one of the wagons giving a
little jump every time he heard hammering. He woke
slowly and saw Elka sitting up in the bed, her fine breasts
softly outlined in the street light which penetrated the
room through a crack between the curtains.

'Who the hell's that!' She swung her feet out of the bed
and groped on the floor for her housecoat.

'Oh, no,' said Sussock, and groaned.

'Do you know who it is, Ray? Do you?' She turned to
him and pushed a clenched fist into the mattress. 'Have
you told anybody about us? I'm angry if you have! Have
you?'

'Fabian Donoghue knows,' he said. 'He got it out of me
with a neat trick.'

'God, Ray!'

'I've asked him to keep it under his hat.'

'I should think so, you ass. Well you'd better let the
smooth bastard in—it's a toss-up whether he brings the
door down before he has a seizure.'

Sussock struggled out of bed and yelled 'All right!' and

the hammering stopped.

'Christ, Sussock, it's five in the bloody morning. What does he want?'

'It'll be the head-banger, Slow Tom, he's struck again; Donoghue told me he'd do this, he said I ought to buy you a phone.'

'I think that's a bloody good idea, Sussock.' She threw down her house coat and pulled the sheets over her, curling into a foetal position. 'And don't forget to turn the bloody light out.'

'Piss off,' said Sussock under his breath. He pulled on his trousers and went to the door to let Donoghue in out of the cold.

Donoghue stepped into the hallway and walked into the kitchen. Sussock went back into the bedroom and brought his clothes in a bundle and dumped them on the red Formica table top.

Red is an odd colour at five in the morning. It hurt Sussock's eyes to look at the kitchen table.

'So it's Slow Tom,' he said, leaning back against the wall, struggling with a sock.

'It is, can't think of any other reason to disturb you and the delectable Elka.'

'Ssh, she'll still be awake.'

Donoghue whispered, 'Sorry,' and then said, 'Anyway, time enough for that later. Right now I need you.'

'There's some compensation, I suppose.' He reached for his shirt. 'No time for a wash?'

'Don't see why not, Ray, we're not going to stop anything tonight.'

Sussock dropped his shirt and went into the bathroom. Donoghue stood at the door.

'It's an old woman this time, well, sixty-odd, anyway,' said Donoghue, enjoying the steam which played about his face. He wished he'd allowed himself the luxury of a shave. 'He got into her house.'

'Inside the house!' said Sussock through a layer of lather. 'She must have known him.'

'That's what I think; this could be the break we need. Press on, Ray.'

'All right, you said I could wash.'

'It was definitely Slow Tom,' Donoghue went on. 'Once in the stomach and once in the neck. Neighbours came home from an all-night party and saw her lying in her hall with tacky black stuff on the floor polish. He left his calling card resting on her coat.'

'Who was she?' Sussock towelled himself and went to get his shirt.

'Lady called Margaret Stewart. Aged sixty-two. Retired nursing sister.'

Outside the snow was driven on a biting east wind. It was a heavy fall, with an inch already covering the windscreen of Donoghue's Rover.

'Careful how you go,' said Donoghue. 'There's three inches of frozen slush under this lot.'

'And I thought the thaw had set in.' Frank Sussock stepped gingerly round the car and opened the passenger door.

Donoghue drove carefully, rarely exceeding twenty-five miles an hour, and on sidelights because the headlights reflected back off the snow and blinded him. Half an hour after leaving Elka Willem's flat in Langside he pulled up at what he judged to be the kerb outside Margaret Stewart's stairway in Hillhead. A constable stood at the close mouth. His cape was white with snow. Donoghue and Sussock showed him their IDs and went up to the second landing. Another constable stood outside the heavy black door, which had 'Stewart' on the front and another sign, 'no hawkers or circulars' underneath. The wood on the door was stained and polished and had a pane of stained glass which showed a sailing ship in a stormy sea. The carpets in the flat had a detailed pattern and were threadbare in places, the furniture was dark and heavy, the light bulbs were small and gave reluctantly. There was a strange smell of carbolic, and each room bristled with order and hygiene. A man with spiky black hair and spectacles brushed the hall furniture for prints.

Margaret Stewart's body had lain on the floor of her hall, on the polished floorboards where the frugal woman had not allowed herself a rug. A chalk outline showed where she had lain. She was found on her side with her legs folded and her arms outstretched. The outline was broken in two places where the drying blood would not allow the passage of chalk.

The flash-bulbs had illuminated the body in series of sharp intense bursts and the photographers had recorded the deceased from the front, the rear, the head and from the feet. There was also a distance shot which showed the position of Margaret Stewart's body in relation to the mahogany wardrobe and the rubber plant by the door. One of the cameras had been a Polaroid, and six photographs lay on the telephone table, left behind for the edification of the Investigating Officer.

'You know what the people on the stair are going to say,' said Donoghue, sifting through the photographs. 'Half are going to say she was the nicest, kindest old lady you could wish to meet, and the other half are going to say she was a crabbit old bitch, and the truth is going to be somewhere in between.'

'Any family?' asked Sussock as Donoghue handed him the photographs.

'No. She was a Miss, and I've a feeling we'll find out that she was a very proper Miss.' He turned to the man who was brushing the furniture with a grey-white powder. 'Anything?'

'Not a thing, sir,' said the man, standing up. He was slightly built and had worked as a laboratory assistant in a comprehensive school before he saw the post of Forensic

Assistant with the Strathclyde Police advertised in the Regional Council Bulletin. 'Not a thing anywhere, sir, clean as a new pin,' he walked a little way toward Donoghue, but was careful to remain at a respectful distance, as he felt befitted a Detective-Inspector. He was also careful not to stand on the chalk outline.

'I don't think he came in very far, sir, there's a bit of mud and slush on the floor by the door; well, there was, it's been trampled a bit; it melted and lost any shape quickly, so we couldn't take any casts. The photographers recorded it, but that was all we could do. I remember the footprints were small, but they were probably hers. She was wearing brogues.'

'She was fully dressed,' said Sussock, holding the photographs. 'A coat, and a hat with a pin through it. So it's not an attack in the early hours of the morning when all good nursing sisters should be in bed.'

'No. She was attacked when she was about to leave the flat or just as she returned,' said Donoghue. 'The water in the hall suggests she had just returned. She's lying facing the door, so she was probably knifed as she turned to shut it behind her.'

'He was waiting for her.'

'Or he followed her in.'

'Who was first here?' asked Sussock.

'King. He was the duty officer.' Donoghue looked at the Forensic Assistant. 'Where's King now?'

The man shrugged his shoulders, and the gesture annoyed Donoghue and made him rethink the good impression the man had first made on him.

'What's your name?' asked Donoghue.

'Bothwell, sir. Jimmy Bothwell.'

'Where's PC King?' Donoghue turned to the constable on the stairs.

'Next landing up, sir,' replied the constable. 'Interviewing the couple who found the body.'

'Well, we can leave him to do a good job. Come on, Ray, let's see what we can dig up.'

Sussock and Donoghue had amassed forty-five years' police work between them and in that time they had been in a lot of rooms in a lot of houses. They had been into rooms which were full of youth and confidence, with pop posters on the walls and with trees painted on the ceilings; they had been into rooms which were full of nothing; the flat personality living there had no use for decoration or ornament. They had been in rooms like Patrick Duffy's, a room which was full of a life of oblivion because reality was so awful, rooms of acute depressives where the walls and even the windows had been painted black. Individually or together they had visited homes in Milngavie, Bearsden, Bridge of Weir, which looked as though they had been prepared for an Ideal Home display, and just as lifeless. Looking into other people's lives never bothered Donoghue or Sussock, but they were upset by Margaret Stewart's bedroom.

There was a high, hard bed with a thick mattress, there was a dresser and a wardrobe and a chest of drawers, all very dark, very solid pieces of furniture. The carpet was dark green with tassles round the edges. There was a painting called 'Loch Lomond with Bluebells' hanging on the wall. It was a room of no ambition left, resignation to life's lot, it was a room of what you have left after it all at the age of sixty-two. Both men knew that they were looking into their futures. They left the room, silently shutting the door behind them.

In the living-room they found Margaret Stewart's diary on a shelf underneath the coffee table. The entry for the 21st of January read:

    9.30 Duty Oxfam Shop
    12.00 Lunch at Meg's
    2.00 Hairdressers/shopping
    7.00 Amnesty International Meeting

Donoghue handed the diary to Sussock. 'Ray, I want you
to look for her address book, it'll probably be near here
somewhere. Make a list of all males with a Glasgow address and see them all. Sooner or later you'll come across
one who was at the A.I. meeting, then you'll be able to
get names of all those others who were at the meeting.
Check them all out. We're looking for a male with light-
coloured hair.'

'I remember,' said Sussock drily.

'That should keep you busy for the rest of the day. You
can take my car back to the station.'

Sussock stooped and rummaged among copies of *People's
Friend* and a box of chocolates and located a slim red
book with a pencil fastened to the spine. He opened it and
nodded to Donoghue. He slipped the book into his coat
pocket and left the flat. Donoghue heard voices in the
hall. It was King talking to Bothwell. 'Living-room,' he
shouted. King came into the room and Donoghue turned
and looked at him, staring at him but not saying
anything. King knew he was expected to start talking but
didn't want to say anything irrelevant, he didn't want to
say anything that Donoghue already knew. In a milli-
second King reasoned that, Donoghue being the man he
was he would have ascertained his whereabouts, and so he
pitched straight into a precis of the interview he had just
conducted with the young and much shaken couple who
lived one flight of stairs up.

'Came home at close on one, sir,' said King, feeling in-
timidated by the tall dapper man in a woollen overcoat
and a fur hat like the ones the Soviet soldiers wear. 'Saw
the door of the flat open, ajar a fraction of an inch. They
were worried because Miss Stewart was usually in bed by
eleven. Very consistent in her habits, Miss Stewart. So
they said, anyway. They were worried because Miss
Stewart wouldn't normally be up and wouldn't have her
door open on account of the weather. So they rang the

doorbell and got no answer and so they pushed the door open and saw the deceased lying in the hall. Then they phoned the police.'

'Was there a light on in the hall?'

'I asked them. They can't recall the light being on but saw the body clearly. It might have been the stair lighting which shone into the flat.'

Donoghue was satisfied with that answer. In a state of excitement or stress people can forget the most obvious things, like whether the light was on or off, or come to the conclusion, for instance, that it was off by the circuitous route of remembering the glow of a luminous clockface. Not remembering the light being on seemed an honest and a faithful answer and Donoghue felt that there was a ninety per cent possibility that the light was off. It might be important. He walked into the hallway. King followed. The light switch was halfway between the front door and the living-room.

'Water inside the door,' said Donoghue. 'Could have been brought in by him or her. What time did the couple upstairs leave for their party?'

'Eight. Eight-thirty.'

'They didn't notice anything unusual on the way out?'

'No, sir.'

'The pathologist will tell us later when she died but we might need to know sooner,' Donoghue mused to himself. 'They didn't notice anything unusual on the way down so we'll assume Miss Stewart to have been out, probably at the A.I. meeting as she had planned.'

'A.I.?'

'Amnesty International. So, she came back, it must have been her feet that brought in the moisture, and he stabbed her as she opened the door and before she could reach the light switch.'

'Would he not have brought some muck in with him?'

'Apparently not. The footprints were small, like a woman's.'

'So he didn't step over the threshold. He stabbed her on the stair.'

'As I said, as she opened the door. Or?'

'Sir?'

'I said, "or?" King. Why else would he not leave foot-marks in the hall, if he came in?'

King had a brief and fantastic vision of a man with a knife suspended above the ground by balloons. 'Well . . .' he said.

'Well?' Donoghue sucked on his pipe. 'Well, perhaps he was waiting for her to come home, sitting on the stairs for up to an hour, with his boots drying nicely.'

'That means he was known to her.'

'Uh-huh. Sergeant Sussock has the address book at the moment.'

'What a way to go,' said King.

Sussock drove back to P Division. In the early morning snow the building's lights affected him like a lighthouse, or a home fire. Sussock didn't know which, but he felt better for seeing them glowing in the darkness. He had had no breakfast and a working man needs food and hot drink. In a small room, which contained four tables, chairs, a three-ring cooker and a fridge, and which was optimistically known as 'the canteen', Sussock made himself toasted cheese pieces and a mug of coffee. He sat down with his breakfast, an open notebook, and the late Margaret Stewart's address book. He made a list of all males with a Glasgow address and worked out a route which he would take to visit each. It was 7.15 a.m. He needed co-operation and he wouldn't get it by knocking people out of comfortable beds, not on a morning when the snow could be measured in tons per square yard, and ten degrees below could be considered warm. He put his feet up and went to sleep.

Donoghue hitched a lift in an area car back to P Division. There are ninety-seven persons employed at P Division, from Findlater down to young Gus, recently recruited into the maintenance team, and there's the ninety-eighth person, who can get away with leaving dirty cups in the sink, the lighting on (despite 'save it' stickers), and who always walks away from the toilet without flushing it. Donoghue rolled up his sleeves and washed the dirty mug, and the plate which had once held a slice of toast. He made himself a coffee and carried it to the incident room. The duty constable stood as he entered. Donoghue waved him down and picked up the phone. It was 8.30 a.m.

'Press agency?' asked Donoghue, holding the receiver in one hand and his coffee in the other.

'The very same,' said the voice down the phone.

'Inspector Donoghue, P Division,' said Donoghue. 'We've some business for you. About the head-banger.'

'That so?' The press agency had offices in Ingram Street near the Sheriff Court. They could telex the news to all the local and national papers in a matter of minutes and net themselves a handsome percentage in the process. Donoghue preferred press conferences, he liked the press to feel involved, he was continually wooing them because he never knew when he'd need their co-operation. But when a bulletin had to be out urgently he needed the agency.

'That's so,' he said.

'How about the code word?'

'Moment,' said Donoghue. He indicated to the duty constable to pass him a strong metal box which stood on a shelf in the room. The constable handed it to Donoghue and Donoghue nodded to the constable to leave the room. He took a keyring from his pocket, and selected a chunky key, unlocked the box. He took a printed card from the box and said, 'My Fair Lady.'

'Bang on,' said the voice. 'What news from the shires?'

'Slow Tom struck again last night, retired nursing sister, spinster, lived in the West End.'

'He's establishing a pattern, this guy,' said the voice.

'Yes, she was murdered around midnight, that fits with the pattern too.'

'She could have been knocked off yesterday night?'

'Could have.'

'Code for yesterday, please.'

'Come on!'

'That's not right.'

'You know what I mean.'

'That's not it either. Listen, I reckon there's enough on with one nutter out there, we can't have anybody ringing in and telling us Her Maj. is being measured for the wooden box.'

'O.K.' said Donoghue, running his index finger along the printed sheet. 'Yesterday was Chorus Line. I don't know how you think them up.'

'We work them out in slack times. After stage shows we're having famous explorers—you know, Livingstone, Ericson, that should see us to the end of the winter. Keep that under your hat.'

'I will.'

'So she was murdered late last night or early this morning. Definitely the work of Slow Tom.'

'Definitely.' Donoghue shut the box and locked it. 'She was murdered in her house.'

'In the house!'

'Right. I want you to play that up, although he was likely waiting on the stair for her or came to the door with her and stabbed her just after she had opened it.'

'All right. Any name?'

'Not yet, we're tracing relatives.'

'I'll get right on it.'

'Thanks,' said Donoghue and hung up.

He went to his office and consulted the diary. The tape was the subject of his morning's work. At 9.30 a graphologist was expected from the university who would, Donoghue hoped, give some insight into the psyche of the man who wrote the note. At breakfast at the North British Hotel (at the expense of Strathclyde Regional Council) was an expert in regional accents who had travelled up from Sheffield on the night sleeper (also at the expense of Strathclyde Regional Council). He was expected at P Division (escort provided) at 11 a.m.

The graphologist was a portly middle-aged man in tweeds who, to Donoghue, had an Edwardian appearance. He carried himself with a certain self-important pomp into Donoghue's office, and taking Donoghue's hand, sat down without first being asked.

'I wonder if I could ask you to sign the Official Secrets Act, Mr Simpson,' said Donoghue. 'It's to . . .'

'I know what it's for, young man. There's no need, I'm already bound by it.'

'I didn't know that.'

'Probably because I signed the Act,' said Simpson. 'It's nothing top secret; if you must know I help the M.o.D. weed out the unsuitables among their applicants.'

'Oh,' said Donoghue, sliding the paper back into his desk drawer. 'Well, I have photocopies of a letter and the envelope which contained it.' He handed the two pieces of paper to Simpson and reached for his pipe. He needed a lot of co-operation from Mr Simpson of the Applied Psychology Department and he needed it yesterday. Donoghue knew academics to be a whole bunch of queer birds, divorced from reality, the only currency they understood being brain power. You can tell an academic he's kind, Donoghue had once said to Sussock, you can compliment him on his personal courage or resilience, his wife can feed him *cordon bleu* for a month but you'll never reach him unless you get down on your knees and worship his brain. Donoghue thought that the only way to get rapid co-operation from Simpson was to relate to him as though he was the best thing that had happened to psychology since Adler.

'I appreciate you have to study these samples at greater depth, Dr Simpson,' said Donoghue, beginning the homage by awarding Simpson a Ph.D., 'But frankly I would find your immediate reaction invaluable, sir.'

'Well, m'boy.' Simpson inched forward on his chair and rested his right hand on his right knee. 'You're right, I'll have to take these back to the department and have a close look at them, because they are not at all what I expected to see, not at all.'

'No?'

'Not at all. You see, I would have expected this Slow Tom character to have thin spiky handwriting, possibly with arty decorations round the edge of the paper and big gaps between the letters of the same word and in other places the letters of different words running into each other.

'But not this fellow, he's not got normal writing—what I would call normal—it's outside the wide mainstream of adult handwriting but yet it isn't grossly abnormal. At first glance it looks not unusual, but look at it closely; the big loop of the letters, strong, carefully constructed characters, all upright, the detached capital "I". It's like a child's writing.'

'Mm,' Donoghue took his pipe from his mouth. 'It's not a child, though, Dr Simpson, we have his voice on tape and he seems an accomplished guitar-player. Would you like to hear the tape?'

'No, it wouldn't help me. The name he's chosen for himself is childlike; "Slow Tom" sounds like a character from a child's story book: "Slow Tom", the friendly snail who lives under the woodshed. Certainly doesn't go with the sort of personality who leaps out of the shadows and stabs people.'

'No insight?' said Donoghue.

'None. He's playing a game.'

'That's the impression I have. Would he be a university student?'

'Wouldn't think so. It's easier to get in now than it was in my day. He certainly wouldn't be a psychology student, he could be an engineer. You know the old joke, "Before I came to university I couldn't spell engineer, now I are one." I think there's a lot of truth in that, Inspector. But even then . . .'

Donoghue smiled, but only because he thought protocol so dictated.

Simpson folded the two pieces of paper into his jacket pocket and shook Donoghue's hand and promised a written report in two or three days. Donoghue thanked him and walked with him to the entrance of the building. They shook hands again and Simpson stepped out into the blizzard.

Montgomerie was beginning to feel hungry. The basement room he and Gillian had crept into the previous night was cluttered with bric-a-brac, old photographs and odd pieces of furniture with a curtain hanging in front of the washbasin. They had slept in a thin and uncomfortable bed pushed against a damp wall. He knew he should be out working, tramping the reading-rooms and libraries, attending the lunchtime meetings, looking for blondie with the box. But outside it was cold, he was lying with a sleeping girl, he was warm, and wasn't this what young bodies are for? He closed his eyes again: he could never cope with guilt.

But there was a pain at the top of his stomach which pestered and nagged and wouldn't go away. He stirred and groaned and yawned in an attempt to wake Gillian. At 10.30 he was due to phone Donoghue.

Gillian moved a little and nestled her shoulder into his

armpit and her head rested on his chest. What did a man have to do to get fed around here? Me Tarzan, you Jane. Tarzan needs munchies. He decided to tickle her gently, and stopped just before she woke up.

'Hi,' she smiled and reached up to kiss his beard. 'Sleep well?'

'Like a babe.'

'Mmm, man.' She ran her hand over his chest. 'Would you like some breakfast, Mal?'

'Let me get it for you.'

'No, I'll do it. I'd like to get it for you.'

'I'd like to get it for you.'

'You're my guest, I'll get it.'

'O.K.,' said Montgomerie.

At ten thirty-five with three cups of coffee and a bowl of hot muesli inside his stomach and 'see you later' ringing in his ears he left the house and walked down the street to the public phone box. The voice in his ears worried him. There was one problem about breaking records: you get tangled up in the finishing-tape.

'Your time is ten thirty,' said Donoghue. 'Not ten thirty-eight.'

'Yes, sir,' said Montgomerie. He adjusted his watch, which had shown 10.36.

'Where were you last night?'

'Sir? What time?'

'All last night.'

'In the refectory, the university folk club, the television room, then to a student-type pub.'

'Yes, I can imagine. Where were you around midnight?'

'In bed.'

'So you'd left the West End by then?'

Montgomerie didn't say anything.

'Do you know where Otago Street is in Hillhead?'

'Yes, sir. In fact, I'm phoning from the call box at the

bottom of that street.' In fact he had spent the night in the basement of No. 86, sir.

'A lady called Margaret Stewart, first floor, No. 88, had a visit from Slow Tom last night, about midnight, probably earlier. I gather you didn't see anything suspicious before you left for home?'

'No, sir. Wild night, hardly saw anything.'

'What are your movements today?'

'Jazz club tonight. I'll spend the day in the library reading-room.'

'And the pub, no doubt,' said Donoghue. 'Don't forget to charge it up.' He put the phone down.

Montgomerie walked back up Otago Street and saw a constable standing at the close mouth of the stair neighbouring the one where Gillian had a flat. If he had looked round when he left the building he would've seen the constable, but he didn't, he had turned right and hurried to the call box because he knew he was late and didn't like angry Detective-Inspectors.

'Morning, sir,' said the constable, grinning.

'Sod you,' said Montgomerie.

'Nice girl,' said the constable. 'The one that came out of 86 and stood in the snow watching you walk away. She walked past me with her head in the clouds, nice round eyes and a smile that would melt an iceberg.'

'Didn't do much for the snow.'

'Can't make the snow stand still.'

'Listen, Phil,' said Montgomerie. 'I could argue I was integrating with the community but I don't fancy my chances. There's a whole bar full of lager for you and a crate of sherry for the good Lady Hamilton if this is the first time you've seen me today.'

'Have a good journey in, sir,' said Hamilton. He raised his wrist. 'It's ten forty-five, sir, mind how you go, sir, slippy underfoot.'

Montgomerie walked into the wind-blown snow, chastened.

The expert in regional accents from Sheffield University was shown into Donoghue's office by the bemused sergeant at one minute past eleven. He was twenty-eight and introduced himself as 'Sam Payne'. He wore a leather jacket, wide-bottomed denim jeans with cowboy boots for the snow. He carried recording equipment on his shoulder, he had a red and yellow Anti-Nazi-League badge clipped to his jacket zip, he sucked on an empty corncob pipe and had what Donoghue thought the ladies would call 'a beautiful smile.'

'Good morning, Mr Payne,' said Donoghue, extending his hand.

'Sam. Good morning, sir.' He had a firm but not an insensitively crushing grip.

'Sam,' said Donoghue. He would remain either 'Inspector' or 'sir'. He definitely would not be 'Fabian'. This was office hours. 'Take a seat, Sam. I see you take a pipe.'

'Aye, I bought it in a sale in Sheff. Paid 92p for it. Don't know why 92, 90 or a straight quid I could understand, but not 92.'

'Will you try some of this?' Donoghue passed his tobacco across his desk. 'It's a special blend made up by a tobacconist in the city.'

'Sweet-smelling,' said Sam Payne, running his fingers through the strands.

'It has a Dutch base for taste, with a twist of dark shag to give a deeper flavour and slow the burning rate.'

Donoghue watched Sam Payne clumsily fill his pipe. He guessed it was the young man's first pipe and he was reminded of his own first pipe, given to him at the age of fourteen shortly after his father had found a packet of cigarettes hidden in the garden shed.

'You don't like the Nazis, Sam?' asked Donoghue,

lighting his own pipe.

'Never met any to dislike, sir.' Sam Payne struck a match adeptly and Donoghue guessed that Sam had recently switched from cigarettes to a pipe. He thought the change suited, he couldn't visualize Sam Payne with a fag in the corner of his mouth. 'Bit before my time, the war,' said Sam, 'but you don't have to go through a war to dislike Fascism.'

'Are policemen Fascist, Sam?'

'Probably not at the moment, I reckon we're both on the same side with this nutter, but next time there's a National Front rally in Sheff I'll be screaming along with the other thugs, layabouts, Bolsheviks, terrorists and no-good commies.'

Donoghue grinned. 'What's in the bag?'

'Recording equipment and some tapes of Clydeside accents. I thought I might need a comparison.'

Donoghue grunted, reached into his desk drawer, and took out a piece of printed paper. 'Would your political point of view prevent you signing the Official Secrets Act, Sam?'

'I've never done that before.'

'It's the most widely signed Government form, every civil servant has to sign one and people who have access to Government secrets. It's had a lot of flak thrown at it in recent years because it makes people risk prosecution if they reveal something they morally feel that the public should know.'

'Ah, ha,' said Sam Payne.

'What it means is that any information you hear regarding these crimes must be kept to yourself until we close the case.'

'Which may be never. You don't always catch nutters. I read it up before I came here, psychopaths mature at thirty-five, that means they stop killing and live normally, but don't feel any remorse because they haven't any guilt feelings.'

Donoghue made no comment on this crash course in psychology.

'It will be closed; if we don't catch him it'll be closed fifty years from now when his natural lifespan will be presumed to have run out. But anyway we never know, this one could be as old as sixty, although he doesn't sound it. All this form is is a deterrent to stop you printing an account of your trip to Glasgow in the Sheffield whatever-it-is.'

'Star,' said Sam. 'O.K., I'll sign it and put it down to an existentialist experience.'

Donoghue pushed the pale yellow piece of paper across his desk and Sam Payne scribbled on it.

'We have to censor the information in case we start a spate of ghost-crimes,' said Donoghue, slipping the paper back into the drawer. He brought up the cassette player and began pressing buttons.

'Shall we put it in mine?' said Sam Payne. He lifted his machine on to the desk, dull chrome, knobs and dials. 'We'll get better reproduction.'

Donoghue handed him the cassette.

'Eight hundred pounds,' said Sam Payne, sliding the cassette into his machine.

'What?'

'That's how much it cost.' He spun the tape. 'You were looking gone-out, so I told you what I reckoned you must have been asking yourself.'

'Thank you,' said Donoghue. He never knew his thoughts showed so clearly.

Sam Payne pressed a button and the voice, richer than before, said, 'So it's Fabian, is it . . . ?' The two men sat back, pulling on their pipes and listening to the tape. Donoghue moved only once; turning and inclining his head, he glanced out of the window. The blizzard had

obliterated the skyline. When the tape finished Sam
Payne reached forward and pressed another button.

'Good guitar player,' he said, rewinding the spool. 'Immature, as well. Funny, that.'

'Oh?'

'Well, this is Sammy Payne's potted psychology, but I
would reckon those two things don't usually go together.'

'You mean good guitar playing is done only by those
who are old enough to have put in the practice?'

'That's one reason, but I was thinking that practising
takes effort; immature personalities are not capable of
effort, says I.'

'Why do you think he's immature, Sam? Sorry, Sam, I
take a cup of coffee at eleven. Would you care for a cup?'

'Thank you. Well, again you'd have to check this with a
psychologist, but have you noticed anything about his
speech?'

'Middle class, Scottish,' said Donoghue, picking up the
telephone.

'We'll come on to that, but this is off the top of my
head and might be bull, but have you noticed how slowly
he talks? He's rolling those words round his mouth like
he's having it off with them, he's not having any problems
forming the words, he's not dim-witted, he just likes attention and one way of getting attention in speech if you
haven't anything interesting to say is to take five times as
long as everybody else to say each word. So, Sam Payne
says he's immature.'

'Hello, pot of coffee and two cups please, and the first
edition if you've got it in yet.' Donoghue replaced the
receiver. 'That's a sound theory. How do you account for
the guitar-playing?'

'He's a natural. I've been splitting my fingernails on
guitar strings for six years now and I can't even dream
about reaching his standard. He sounds young, so I
presume he popped into this world with his left hand

moving backwards and forwards and his right hand going up and down, just waiting for a guitar to be put in there. He plays superb twelve-bar blues.'

'All right, that tells us something. How about the accent, Sam?'

'Time to earn my keep, is it?' Sam Payne smiled. 'Well, I presumed you'd want an answer as soon as possible, so rather than listen to the tape and give my opinion and then take it back to rainswept Sheff for closer examination, I thought I'd bring my box of goodies to you.'

'Thoughtful of you. Rainswept? It's not snowing down there?'

'No. This is localized, thankfully.'

'How long will you need, Sam?'

'Two hours; I've got tapes of all the greater Glasgow accents, so I shall be able to identify his.'

There was a knock at the door. A constable brought the coffee in. The first edition of the *Evening Times* lay on the tray. Sam Payne smiled at the constable.

'He is Greater Glasgow, is he?'

'I think so. But, like you said, he's middle-class modified accent.'

'Like a first-generation graduate?'

'Yes, or someone who's made it from the factory floor to the boardroom. We never quite make the transition, and so end up with a tongue in both camps. So with this nutter I've got to listen to what's behind the social climbing bit and try and pin down an area.'

'How close can you get?'

'With a good sample we could get down to a town, or a particular valley or coastal region for instance. A lot depends on words used, order of use, as well as pronunciation. But there's not a lot here and, like we've agreed, it's modified.'

'I didn't know that there were so many different accents,' said Donoghue, pouring the coffee.

'Aye, well, there are forty-four identifiable in Yorkshire alone. We don't know how many there are in Scotland because we keep discovering new ones in the Highlands and Islands and we also lose accents as communities die, but we think there're about a hundred and sixty. Also, they change through time. A Greenock accent now wouldn't be the same as a Greenock accent a hundred years back.'

'Well, I'll let you get on with it, Sam.' Donoghue rose from his chair. 'If anyone looks in for me or phones me, I'm in the incident room.' He picked up the paper and held it up for Sam Payne to read the headlines.

They read:

SLOW TOM CLAIMS NUMBER FOUR
FIVE MORE TO GO?

'Doesn't mess around, this lad,' said Sam Payne, and slipped the headphones over his ears.

CHAPTER 6

If Ray Sussock thought he'd struck pay-dirt with his first call, he reckoned he'd found the mother-lode with his fourth. The route he had worked out in the canteen at P Division, after eating his toasted piece and before taking a nap, had concentrated on the West End of the city. In fact, discounting addresses in other parts of the country and overseas addresses, Margaret Stewart's social life seemed to have been contained in the square mile centering on Byres Road. This was good news for a policeman who had twenty-two calls to make and a bitch-of-a-dog day to make them in. Ordinarily he would have used his car but the weather being the weather, snow being snow, three feet deep in places and still coming, he reckoned his optimum form of transport would be horseback. The

Strathclyde Police had horses, fine chestnut beasts, always finely groomed, but they were not up for grabs as far as the CID were concerned. Sussock fell back on his second optimum form of transport and parked his car near the Western Infirmary and began to walk. The snow had driven most people off the streets and he was alone on Byres Road save for two black figures far ahead of him, struggling against the inclement conditions.

The first call was to a man named Max Gaffney. Max Gaffney was a student of divinity and lived in claustrophobic conditions in a sandstone terrace in the downmarket end of Byres Road. He sat looking at Sussock, holding a mug of coffee in his hands and with two textbooks open in front of him. Sussock evidently frightened him, he thought, either that or Max Gaffney usually talks to people with his knees tucked under his chin and his free hand trying to clasp both ankles. He wore black-framed spectacles with thin lenses.

'Oh, her,' said Gaffney after Sussock, who had drawn a blank when telling him the name of the murdered woman, had described her as he thought she would have looked in life. 'Oh.'

'You know her?'

'Well, yes.'

'Well?'

'No.'

'You said well.'

'I didn't mean it like that.'

'How did you mean it?'

'Not like that like, well, as an expression.'

'How close were you?'

'Not very.'

'Is that why you're not upset, Max?'

'I hardly knew the old dame.'

'How did you know her?'

'Through Amnesty International.' That was pay-dirt

and Sussock took out his notebook. 'All right, Max, I want the names and addresses of all who were at the A.I. meeting last night.'

'We must have been some of the last people to see her alive.'

'That's right. The names, Max.'

'Well there was me, and old Maggie Stewart, there was Dick Finlay, Ollie Grant, Anthea McCabe, Willie Wilson, some girl called Frances, first time I saw her was last night. I don't know where she lives.'

'Last name?'

Gaffney shook his head.

'Carry on.'

'Robin Graff and Marjorie Boyd.'

'Four blokes,' said Sussock to himself.

'Five.' Gaffney sounded hurt. 'I was there.'

'I was discounting you, Max. What are the addresses? Start with Dick Finlay.'

Gaffney reeled off the addresses from memory. Sussock thanked him and left. He didn't think Max Gaffney was the suspect: he was completely bald. What did surprise him about Gaffney was the man's reaction, or lack of it, to the news of the death of someone whose address book he had been in. Gaffney was surprised, a little shocked, but not unduly disturbed. He had the impression that as he shut the door Gaffney's nose would be buried in his books as though his visit had never occurred.

Sussock was to find Gaffney's reaction to be typical and he soon reached the conclusion that Margaret Stewart, spinster, retired nursing sister, was a woman terrified of loneliness. He began to see her, sixty-two years old, sitting on the floor drinking coffee with undergraduates, an old lady telling her grandchildren where they were going wrong, and they listened because they were too polite to do anything else. She was probably so lonely that she invited Slow Tom up for a cup of Horlicks.

In the close mouth of Max Gaffney's stairway Sussock worked through the list Gaffney had given him. Two of the names had been in Margaret Stewart's address book, the rest were new, but all thankfully, were in the West End. Sussock thought he was fortunate there; were it not for his frozen feet and his windblown face and the melting snow trickling down his neck and getting inside his shoes he would have reckoned that his luck was in.

The fourth name on the list was a man called Oliphant Grant. He lived in a sandstone tenement block, similar to Max Gaffney's address. Sussock climbed the stone stairs and knocked the door marked 'Grant'. He knocked again and was about to write this one off as one to be revisited when he heard a sound inside the flat. Ten seconds later Oliphant Grant opened the door and Sussock's blood froze.

Oliphant Grant was a goofy-looking guy with buck teeth. He had ginger hair and scratches on his forehead.

The two men stood staring at each other for fifteen or twenty seconds. Sussock didn't know how to play it: he managed to stay cool. He couldn't have got much colder. He felt the skin on his temples grow taut as he looked at the man.

'Police,' said Sussock. He flashed his ID.

'I know,' said the teeth. 'You look like a pig.'

'How do pigs look?'

'Hard mean bastards with rings through their noses so they can get led around by the Tories.'

'That right?'

'That's right. What do you want, anyway?'

'I want a few answers, Mr Grant. You going to invite me in?'

'Supposing I say no?'

'Then I'll come in anyway and you'll just be another name on the long list of people who've unsuccessfully sued the police for assault.'

Grant eyed him coldly, and then stepped aside.

It was dark inside Grant's flat. The wallpaper was brown and the light was dim. Snow had driven past the window. There was a desk, and a cigarette smouldering in the ashtray. 'So come on,' he said.

'You know an old lady called Margaret Stewart?'

'Yes.' He wasn't giving anything.

'What do you know about her?'

'What do you want to know for?'

'I'm asking the questions.'

'Not so easy, Porky. I'm not one of your Drumchapel drunks that doesn't know his rights.'

'That right?'

'That's right.'

'Cocky bugger, aren't you?'

'Civil liberty's my watchword. Why do you want to question me about old Maggie?'

'That's what you call her, is it?'

'We called her.'

'When was the last time you saw her?'

'Last night. We had a meet about innocents in the pig-pens in South America.'

'What time?'

'From eight till ten. That's two hours.' Sussock let that go.

'Ten o'clock was the last time you saw her?'

Grant nodded and inhaled the cigarette smoke deeply.

'So she left at ten to go home.'

'No, she left at ten to sell her tail in Blytheswood Square. Where the hell do you think she went?'

'Where was the meeting?'

'In a house in Highburgh Road.'

'She walked from Highburgh Road to Otago Street last night? Some night for a walk.'

'Not many taxis around. Anyway, someone went half-way with her.'

'Who?'

'Lassie did, some girl called Anthea. Anyway, old Maggie was so desperate to be part of something she'd walk across the North Pole if there was a cup of tea and a chat at the end of it.'

'She'd have to be desperate to want your company, sonny.'

'What do you mean by that?'

'Friendly sort of bloke, aren't you?'

'So, I don't like the polis.'

'Spend a lot of time in, do you?'

'None of your business.'

'We'll see about that.'

'Old Maggie been complaining about me?'

'Should she?'

'She doesn't like my language. I tend to profane, but I've kept it clean with you because I only swear at the people I like.'

'She hasn't been making any complaints. She's dead.'

Grant smiled thinly, and Sussock wanted to put his hand across Grant's face. 'So the old biddy's finally bought it. Who did it?'

'How do you know someone did anything, Oliphant?'

'Well, I . . .'

'Yes?'

'Don't unnerve me, save your cheap tricks for the thickies, cop.'

'I'm waiting, Oliphant.'

'Mr Grant.'

'I'm still waiting.'

'Shit. I mean, would you come asking questions if she'd broken her neck?'

'Might. Old question, Grant. Did she fall or was she pushed?'

'Someone knocked her off?'

'Uh-huh.'

'So why interrogate me?' He pulled on his cigarette.

'Nice head of hair you got there, Mr Grant. Always been that colour, has it?'

'What do you mean?'

'What happened to your forehead?' Sussock touched his own forehead. 'The scratches?'

'Me and this holly bush had a fight.'

'Tell me about the holly bush.'

'Why?'

'Because I asked you nicely.'

'Who killed Margaret Stewart?' He was suddenly alarmed.

'That's what I'm trying to find out.'

'How did she die?'

'Knifed. Very nasty.'

'Was it the head-banger, Slow Tom? Listen, you don't think I . . . I mean, my hair. I'm not under suspicion, am I?'

'Damn right you are!' snarled Sussock. 'Tell me about the holly bush.'

'I tripped on the ice a couple of days back and fell headfirst into a shrubbery.'

'Do you expect me to believe that?'

'No, you people believe what you want to believe.'

'Why did you kill her, Oliphant?'

'I didn't kill fucking nobody.'

'You got an alibi: for last night—after the meeting?'

'No. But that means fucking nothing.'

'Profaning, is it? Does that mean I'm growing on you, Oliphant?'

'Fuck off.'

'You have a knife, do you?'

'No. Well I have . . . a camping knife. I go hiking.'

'Get your coat, Ollie—is that what your friends call you? You and me are going for a chat in a nice cosy pig-pen. We'll do our best to make you feel at home.'

'I'm not going anywhere.'

'Yes you are, you're assisting the police with their enquiries like any public-spirited citizen. You're doing it entirely of your own volition. Get your coat.'

'You have to be joking. I'm not shifting.'

'You want me to arrest you?'

'Yes, I want you to arrest me. Then I can sue for a wrongful arrest.'

'Have you got it wrong, Oliphant!'

'*Mr* Grant. No, I got it right. If I go with you of my own free will there's no limit to the time you can keep me in there, beating me up, kicking me to hell in the cells. You arrest me, pig, and charge me, then we both know the game we're playing.'

Sussock sighed. Grant had a point, he had to concede that, but the boy also had a lot to lose. 'Let me spell it out for you, Grant,' said Sussock, patiently. 'We arrest you because you fit the bill and you can't provide an alibi for last night. Then we charge you with murder. Then you spend the weekend in the cells, then it's the Sheriff Court on Monday and you'll be remanded, and don't even pray for bail; further appearances before the Sheriff, further remand, then it's the trial, if you're innocent then you go free, if not you go up for life. If you can't tell me where you were after ten last night . . .'

'I can tell you.'

'Where?'

'Here.'

'Alone?'

'All alone.'

'Not good enough, Mr Grant. How about the nights of the 16th, 17th and 18th of January?'

'Do you know, I can't remember?'

'Anyway, if you come with me we'll scratch your back, nice ride home in a car, for instance.'

'If you let me go.'

'Aye. If we let you go. Listen, you'll never sue us for wrongful arrest on this one and either way you're coming to have a chat with my governor. So why don't you make it easy on yourself?'

'I've a lecture at three.'

'Are you coming or am I going to arrest you?'

'You're going to arrest me.'

Sussock pulled his radio out of his coat pocket and requested a car in connection with an arrest. He sat down, Oliphant Grant sat down opposite him and lit another cigarette. The two men sat staring at each other and Sussock noticed that the skin on Grant's hands was wrinkled and mottled like those of an old woman. Oliphant Grant was twenty-two and fate hadn't been kind to him.

Two constables arrived ten minutes after Sussock had radioed in. Sussock stood as they entered the room. 'Oliphant Grant,' he said. 'I arrest you for the murder of Margaret Stewart on or about the night of the 21st of January. You are not obliged to say anything but anything you do say will be taken down and may be given in evidence.'

Grant sat silently and motionless. The two constables picked him up and bundled him down the stairs into the area car. Sussock got in the front seat.

Sussock knocked on Donoghue's door and walked into his office. His jaw dropped. Sam Payne took the headphones from his head. 'Incident room,' he said with a smile. Sussock found Donoghue sitting on the table leafing through the post-mortem report on Margaret Stewart. Sussock told him about Oliphant Grant.

'Where is he?' Donoghue put down the report. The duty constable looked up with interest.

'Cells,' said Sussock.

Oliphant Grant was sitting on the bunk with his knees

held together. There was a toilet without a seat in the corner.

'I want my trousers,' said Grant.

'Sorry,' said Donoghue. 'It's in case you hang yourself. We have to take care of you. We'd've had your tie if you'd been wearing one.'

'So when does the heavy stuff start?'

'Don't know what you mean, son,' said Donoghue.

'You know, lead shot inside hose-pipes, kneeling on the spleen.'

'You've been reading too many story books, son.'

'He's been cautioned,' said Sussock.

'Excellent. I like to do things by the book. You're allowed one phone call, Grant.'

'Who do I call?'

'I thought you knew the rules,' Sussock said with malice.

'Anyone you like, Grant,' said Donoghue. 'But most people call their solicitor.'

'I don't have one.'

'We have a list upstairs. Do you want to make a phone call?'

Grant nodded.

'Sergeant, please give the prisoner his trousers and escort him upstairs to the front desk where he will make one phone call to a solicitor which he will choose from the list you will make available to him.'

Sussock said, 'On your feet, Grant.' He flung the man's trousers at him.

Donoghue didn't like cells and he stepped outside when Grant had left. He stood next to a young constable, but moved off when he noticed the young man fidgeting nervously, and waited at the entrance to the cell corridor. Grant returned, escorted by Sussock. He was looking sullen and arrogant. Donoghue heard Sussock yelling at Grant to get his trousers off and when he saw them being flung into the corridor he entered the cell.

'What did your solicitor say?' asked Donoghue.

'He asked me if I was guilty.'

'What did you say?'

'What do you think I said, piggy?'

'I think you probably said yes, and if you said no then I'd say you were lying.'

'He said no,' said Sussock.

'Did he, indeed?'

'Why did you say no?' asked Sussock.

'Why the hell do you think I said no?'

'Like killing, do you?'

'Flies and the like, aye.'

'Tell us what you were doing last night after the meeting.'

'Charge me, pig.'

'Patience. We have to question you first. Don't rush your fences, laddie.'

'Like a game, is it?' sneered Grant.

'Oh, aye,' said Sussock, clenching his fist.

Donoghue tapped Sussock on his arm and indicated the corridor. They walked out of the cell. Grant started laughing and making an oink, oink sound.

Down the corridor, away from the cell, Donoghue said, 'He's not our man.'

'How no'?'

'Wrong voice. Even allowing for accidental or deliberate distortion on the tape, he's not the same guy that sent us a rendering of his song. He's innocent anyway—he doesn't feel guilty. I can sense guilt, Ray, no matter how a person is acting or what he's saying, calm or panic-stricken, the guilt comes out. Grant is not our man.'

'He fits the description, he's a right-hander with light-coloured hair and there's scratches on his forehead. And he can't give an alibi.'

'And he's got a king-sized chip on his shoulder. Careful how you go in there, Ray, he wants you to lay one on him. He wants to be victim to some police brutality; he's doing his best to get under your skin.'

'He's succeeding.'

'Don't let him. You'll just make him a martyr. Have a constable in the cell with you, remember he's there, that'll be enough to stop you bouncing Grant's head off the wall. You have enough to keep him, Ray, and I'll back you as far as you want to take it. You have to follow it through, anyway, until he realizes he's going to lose his game and he gives you an alibi. He'll have one and we can't let him go until we get one that can be verified.'

'Little bastard.'

'Easy, Ray. Did you tell him what you were enquiring about?'

'We got round to it eventually.'

'So he knows we're after Slow Tom?'

'Yes.'

'Did you ask him for alibis for the other nights?'

'Yes.'

'He couldn't give an alibi?'

'He wouldn't. It wasn't so much what he said, more his manner.'

'I've noticed. Anyway, you've won. We haven't got the head-banger but you've a cast-iron case for wasting police time. Keep that at the back of your mind, Ray, and don't let him get the better of you.'

'He won't. Not now.'

'Let him stew for a couple of hours, Ray. Go and take a rest before you go out again, you're probably dropping. You out with the delectable Elka tonight?'

'If I don't fall asleep.' Sussock smiled his appreciation and called the constable out of the cell. He locked Oliphant Grant inside and went to the canteen. He fell asleep at a table with his head resting on his arms.

In the cell next to Grant was a man called Owen Morgans. He was fifty-three, he came from Senghennydd and had lived as a sales representative in Glasgow for three years. Owen Morgans was whimpering. Upstairs Elka Willems and a fourteen-year-old girl called Tracy Mortimer were talking about Owen Morgans.

'There weren't any witnesses, Tracy. How do we know you're telling the truth?'

'I am, I am.' Her handkerchief could have been wrung dry.

'Girls who've been attacked don't calmly follow the man and take the number of his car.'

'I did it because I thought you'd help me.'

'He could get into serious trouble, Tracy, he hasn't done this before.'

'He's probably not been caught before.'

'Tell me how it happened.'

'I've told you three times.' Tracy Mortimer blew her nose.

'Tell me four times.' Elka Willems sat back in her chair and showed no emotion.

'It happened so quickly.'

'We have all day. Have you seen the man before?'

'No, never.'

That might be lie No. 1 of an adolescent fantasy. Owen Morgans sold a quarter of a million pounds' worth of office equipment to Tracy Mortimer's father and had been invited to the Mortimer household for drinks. Tracy had been there, he said, it was just a tale told by a schoolgirl, he said, she may as well have fingered her dentist or maths teacher.

But alone in the cell he began to wring his hands.

'You've never seen him before?'

'No.'

'Think!'

Tracy Mortimer began to cry again. When her father

had brought Owen Morgans home it had been late at night. Tracy had been riding all day and had put in extra hours at the stable, she was tired and about to go to bed. She might have said a bleary-eyed 'hello' without really looking at Owen Morgans, she might never have seen him at all, or she might have seen him and taken a strong fancy to him because he was not an unsightly figure of a man by any means. Owen Morgans's highly successful life might be about to be ruined because of Tracy Mortimer's wishful thinking.

'Tracy, I'm waiting.'

'What for?'

'For you to tell me what happened.'

'I can't, I can't.'

'You will!'

'I've told you already, I thought you'd help me, I thought the police were my friends.'

'Tracy.'

'All right, all right . . .' she blew her nose again. 'I told you, I was walking home, about three o'clock, I'd been at the stables with Veronica, I walked through the woods between Bearsden and Milngavie.'

'The woods would be thick with snow, Tracy. You walked home on the road and this is a pack of lies.'

'No!' Tracy Mortimer thumped the table with two clenched fists, her cheeks shook. 'No, no, we'd been riding in the woods, the paths were trampled clear and it wasn't snowing. There wasn't any snow until today.'

That was true. She'd said that the last time and Elka Willems hadn't been able to shake her.

'Why weren't you at school?'

'I told you, I told you. I was dogging, truanting . . .'

'I know what dogging means.'

'I was dogging to go to the stables. Some of us do it every few weeks. We get bored with school. My parents both work and leave before I do and if I'm back before them I change into my uniform and they don't know any different. I rang up the school and said I'm Veronica's mother and that she's ill and Veronica did the same for me.'

'Why did you wait until this morning to tell your mother about it?'

'I don't know, I don't know . . . last night I went to bed. I said I was tired. I had a nightmare and started crying. My mother came to my room and I told her about it. I showed her the piece of paper with the car number and she phoned the police.'

That was plausible. Reaction delayed by shock, and Mrs Mortimer corroborates the story.

'So you were walking back through the woods?'

She nodded and pressed her handkerchief against her nose. 'I was about halfway home. There was somebody behind me, I think he must have followed me all the way from the stables . . .'

'Why?'

'Well, because, like I said ten times, there were . . . I didn't see any footprints going off the track and into the woods as I walked up the path.'

'All right.' Tracy Mortimer couldn't be shaken. But it still wasn't clinched.

'I heard a branch break behind me but I didn't turn round, I wanted to run but I was afraid to, for some reason I couldn't run. I did start to walk faster. I've told you all this.'

'Tell me again.'

'Please, do I have to?'

'Yes.'

'Well . . . he must have come up fast because the next thing I knew he's running up behind me, I could hear his breath, panting like a horse, I turned and his coat was open and his thing . . .'

'Thing?'

'You know, between his legs.'

'It's got a name, Tracy. Come on, you've managed it before.'

'Penis.'

'Good girl.'

'Well, it was there and he pushed me on my back into the snow at the side of the track with his hands round my throat so I could breathe a bit but not scream and his other hand tried to pull my riding-trousers down. I was struggling but he was heavy.'

'How did you know it was who you said it was?'

'I just got a glimpse, I thought it was him, that's why I followed him down the track when he was running away. I thought I had to see where he went so the police could catch him. I saw him get into a car, an estate car and I wrote down the number.'

'That was a calm thing for someone who's just been attacked to do, to say nothing of great presence of mind for one so young.'

'Well, I did it.'

'And you just happened to have a pen and notebook on you?'

'Yes; no. I had a biro and some old cloakroom ticket that had been in my jacket pocket for years.'

'But you didn't see him clearly?'

'No.'

'Not clear enough to identify him?'

She shook her head. 'He was pushing my head back most of the time, I could just see the sky through the trees.'

'Go on.'

'It's not easy.'

'Go on!'

'Well . . . he pulled my trousers down a bit but he couldn't get far, I'd crossed my legs, you see, then he sat on me, further up and shoved his hand inside my vest, squeezing really hard . . .' she blew her nose. 'Then he pulled his coat up around him and pulled my head up inside his coat and his thing, penis, was in my face . . .'

'Was it erect?'

'Erect?'

'Limp or stiff?'

'Stiff, hard, I thought I was going to be sick inside the coat, the smell . . .'

'All right, Tracy, that's all, it's over.' Elka Willems reached across the table and squeezed Tracy Mortimer's wrist and pushed a box of tissues over to the girl. Human beings have five senses, some say six, but only fantasize about four. An unsolicited mention of smell was what Elka Willems was waiting for. 'All right, Tracy,' she said again. 'It's over, I'll write this down and you'll have to sign it and then you can go home. Your mum's still outside.'

Tracy Mortimer collapsed forward on to the table and began to heave and tremble. Elka Willems thought that it was more than the attack and her questioning that was making the girl cry.

Ray Sussock woke up and made himself a cup of coffee and carried it with him to Oliphant Grant's cell. Grant looked sullen.

'How's it going, Oliphant?' he said, drinking the coffee.

'Don't I get any?'

'You wouldn't like it, it's pigswill.'

'I thought you'd forgotten me.'

'You didn't like it here all by yourself? You'll get used to it, the nights are the worst, all the lags say that, waking up in the middle of the night and not being able to get back to sleep, it's sheer hell. Anyway, you'll find out. You'll have company in the Bar L, though, but I don't think it's company you want, is it, laddie, it's attention.'

'Look, if I tell you where I was when the first two were killed will you let me go?'

'Probably.'

'I haven't got an alibi for Margaret Stewart's death, but I was home. What were the dates?'

'The sixteenth and seventeenth.'

'Aye, I was in Inverness. I was ill and stayed home. I was late back for term. You can check.' He even smiled.

'I will. They on the phone, your Ma and Da?'

Grant quoted a number and Sussock walked out of the cell. He returned a few minutes later. 'It checks out,' he said. 'You're not Slow Tom.'

'So I can go now?'

'So you stay here now.'

'How come?'

'We're dropping the charge of murder, Grant. But I'm charging you with wilfully wasting police time. You'll spend the weekend in Barlinnie and you'll be up before the Sheriff on Monday morning. When you do get out you'll have a couple of worried parents to sort out.'

'You pig bastard,' said Grant.

'I'll be back later to charge you.' He turned and shut the door. As Sussock walked from Grant's cell he passed the open door of the next cell and heard a man crying. 'Yes, all right . . . I did it . . . I've watched her for days . . . I get these feelings . . .'

Donoghue walked with Sam Payne to the entrance of P Division.

'Well that's as near as I can get, Inspector.'

'Helensburgh, Dumbarton area, you say?'

'Yes, tending west rather than east into Glasgow. Not too far west though, no further than Garlochhead. They tend to roll their "r's" a bit more. The sample you gave me doesn't have a significant "r" roll and the vowels tend to be low-pitched.'

'I'll take your word for it, Sam.'

'So long as you appreciate it's only an opinion. I don't

want to be held responsible if the nutter turns out to come from Motherwell, I'm not infallible.'

'Point taken, Sam. I don't expect the word, or name, "Lissu" means anything to you?'

'Not a thing. I've seen the spelling in the papers; no, I can't say I know what it means. I'll ask around for you, though. So long, Inspector.'

'So long, Sam.'

Donoghue watched the leather-jacketed figure draped with recording equipment walk through the snow to the waiting police car. He was changing his mind about academics, just as earlier that morning he had changed his mind about the attitude of a forensic assistant.

My God, was it only this morning?

Richard King signed off duty and stepped into Sussock's office and glanced through the pending file. On his case-load already, beside his commitment to the Slow Tom investigation, was a gang of car thieves who were knocking off only cars with magnesium alloy wheels and leaving the car on a piece of waste ground—minus the wheels; a string of burglaries, committed by a person who had only two fingers of his right hand; a serious assault and an embezzlement. He had more than enough to cope with, but he liked to know what was coming in. He leafed through the files marked with red tape (for immediate allocation) and his attention was caught by a file on a missing boy, first reported missing Thursday 21st January, the previous night, in fact. The home had been visited, so had places the boy might have been, and he was still missing. It was a hell of a long time for an eleven-year-old-boy to be missing in a snow-bound city. King marked the file out to himself and walked back to his office and locked it in his desk drawer. He didn't realize it, but he was beginning to develop the kind of intuition Donoghue had honed to a fine edge.

Sussock didn't see the last of the males on the list he had compiled from Margaret Stewart's address book until 10 p.m. He had drawn a blank with all of them. They either had alibis or black hair or no hair or were left-handed. No, they none of them knew anyone who had a grudge against the old lady. It was 10.30 when he left the last household, and the snow was swirling down. He got back to Rutherglen at 11.30 and let himself in the back door with a key his wife didn't know he had. He crept inside, feeling guilty for being under his own roof, and took off his shoes and coat. Upstairs he heard his wife say, 'What's that noise, Sammy?' and his son reply, 'Oh, it's only Daddy, Mummy. Don't worry.' Sussock slumped on the sofa, too tired to care. There was still a small glow in the firegrate and a slight heat.

He was thankful for small mercies.

CHAPTER 7

Ray Sussock and Elka Willems were walking arm in arm along the gravel path which wound through the shrubs and which was bordered by lush humus. At their side a stream was spilling freshly into a pond. There were fish in the pond, swimming around giant waterlilies. Palm trees arched above them and two pure white cockatoos sat on the branch of a smaller tree. Sussock loosened his shirt collar. Bach's *Jesu, joy of man's desiring* filled the air.

'You'll have to make a decision, Ray,' said Elka. 'You'll crack up. You can't go on like this.'

'It's a big break, Elka. And not only that. I think to leave would be to admit that it was all my fault.'

'Rubbish.'

'I feel guilty about it.'

'Then you're a silly boy, a stupid wee wean, I've told

you before it's not your fault.'

The cockatoos screeched.

'Then I'll have to leave.'

'You *said* it, Ray.'

'I'll need to rent some place. I'll need to start looking. I'll look on the South Side or up the West End.'

'It's got to be a clean break, Ray, not any interim measure. You, Raymond Sussock, are about to break from your wife and son, you're leaving them the house and responsibility for the mortgage repayments, you are about to burn your boats and break clean. You can do it, Ray.'

'Jesus,' he said.

'But you are doing it for yourself, not for to come and stay with me. Remember I might not be here next year, next year I might have got tired of you and gone with another man. Next year I might be living in another city, because I've been in Glasgow for two years now and next year I might want a change. So you've got to stand on your own two feet from the word go.'

'Don't you think I'm too old?'

'No, a thousand times, no! It's not easy, it's never easy moving and unsettling your life but you've got to do it, Ray. I came up from Stranraer and I didn't know a soul and I hated this city, it was cold and hostile, but I stuck it out and now it's O.K. It's going to be easier for you because you know people and I'll visit you. It'll make a change, me staying at your place, anyway.'

He squeezed her waist. He told her he loved her.

'And I love you.' She pecked his cheek. 'But only if you're strong. As soon as you start to lean on me I'll leave you. There isn't any room for weak men in my life.'

They walked on. The gravel grated under their feet.

'I'm going in this afternoon,' he said, breaking the silence between them. 'I'd like to spend the day with you, but Fabian Donoghue is giving up his weekends and I feel

I ought to be there. Do you understand?'

'Of course I do, Ray. Command is a lonely position and I wouldn't have Fabian's job right now, not for a pension. You have to support him. I've stacks of shopping to do anyway and you'll only get in the way. When will you be back?'

'Early evening.'

They walked around the Winter Gardens once again, slowly, and then into the museum of People's Palace and out to where Sussock had parked his car.

'I went to People's Palace a few months ago,' he said as they were driving away. 'I was filling in a split shift. I found out how Glasgow got its name. It comes from two Celtic words, glas and cu, reckons to mean the place of the heavenly green. It's supposed to be built round the spot where St Mungo met St Columba.'

'That a fact?' she said looking across the white sweep of Glasgow Green to the dereliction of the Barrowland. 'The name don't seem to fit now, do it?'

Richard King drove to Partick. He parked his car against a snow drift in Glassel Road and walked up to the top flat of a dark close. He knocked on the door. Behind him, somewhere in the dark, he could hear water dripping steadily. He heard a noise in the flat and the door swung open, wide, and a woman stood in the entrance. She seemed disappointed to see King. It was the first time that King had set eyes on the woman but he could tell that the last two days had aged her considerably. Her eyes were sunken, and her face creased with worry. King showed her his ID.

'Come in, sir, come in,' said the woman, anxiously stepping aside.

'Mr King,' he said. 'Don't call me "sir", please.'

'Mr King,' said the woman.

A girl ran towards him. She was about eight years old.

She looked up at King and said, 'Have you found him?'

'Not yet, hen,' said King.

Mr McAlpine was standing with a newspaper in one hand. As King entered the room he strode across the carpet to the television and switched it off.

'Mr McAlpine?' asked King.

'Aye.' Ron McAlpine extended his hand and King took it. 'I've been out searching,' said the man, 'walked around these streets and down as far as the river. Been out six, seven, I don't know, eight times. I mean, I can't just sit here.'

'No,' said King. 'I think I'd do the same.'

'Would you like a cup of tea, Mr King?' asked Mrs McAlpine, clasping her hands on her forearms.

'That would be very nice. Thank you.' King accepted the offer only because he knew it would give Mrs McAlpine something to do.

'Please sit down, Mr King,' said Ron McAlpine. 'We can't think where he'd be. I've been to all his friends' houses , I've even phoned my brother in Aberdeen in case he's taken it into his head to go visiting. Nothing. Nowhere; nothing.'

'Is he likely to have gone off without telling you?'

'No. It's not his way. He's not an adventurous sort of lad, Ronald. Bit middle-aged, if you see what I mean?'

'I don't, I'm afraid.'

'Set habits, set routes, set routine. Totally predictable.'

'He hasn't done this before, then?'

'No. Never, not ever.'

'He's not gone before,' said the girl. King wanted to pick her up and hold her, he wanted to tell her about all the good things in life, he wanted to tell her that brothers don't go missing, that brothers don't disappear in snow-bound cities which are grinding to a halt, and that they don't stay away for two nights when the temperature drops to fifteen below. He wanted to tell her that what he

feared deep inside wouldn't really be so, and that they
would all be together for Burns Night. Christ, oh merci-
ful Christ, there were times when he hated his job. All he
could say was, 'Have you any idea where he might be,
hen?'

The girl shook her head vigorously.

'Where did he go on Thursday evening, Mr McAlpine?'

'To the youth club, same as always. The one in the
church hall. A game of pinball, a game of indoor foot-
ball, a chat with the lassies. It's run by the minister.'

'He didn't say he was going anywhere after the club?'

'Och, no; on a night like Thursday? I'm surprised he
went out at all. Anyway, the club finishes at 9.30, he's
supposed to be in bed by 10. He wouldn't have gone anywhere after the club.'

'Was he at the club?'

'Oh, yes, yes.'

'Did he leave alone?'

'He left with one other boy, but they would have parted
soon after leaving the church hall. The minister will tell
you.'

'Yes, we already have a statement from him, but I'll see
him again.'

Mrs McAlpine entered the room and handed him a cup
of tea. The cup and saucer rattled in her hand.

'It's the cold that worries me,' she said in a shaking
voice. 'I'm sure it wouldn't be so bad if it was summer-
time. But I lie in my bed at night and listen to the snow
falling off the roof and see the fresh falls in the morning . . .
if only I knew he was warm.'

Her husband put his arm around her. The little girl
ran into her bedroom and shut the door behind her.

'Nothing was worrying him?' asked King.

'No, nothing,' said Ron McAlpine. 'Nothing that we
know about.'

'Would he have told you if there was something bothering him?'

'Yes, I'm sure he would,' said Mrs McAlpine, wiping her cheeks. 'I'm sorry, Mr King.'

'Don't worry about it.' King took a photograph from his jacket pocket. 'Is this the most recent photograph you have of him?'

'That's the one I gave to the other officer, yes. It was taken at Christmas, the jumper he's wearing, the red one, it was a Christmas gift.'

'His hair is like that, is it?'

'Aye,' said Ron McAlpine. 'A bit of ginger sticking out of the black. He got teased about it.'

When King left, Ron McAlpine saw him to the door. 'Thank you, sir, thank you,' he said.

King walked down the stair and stood at the close mouth. He looked at the drifts, he looked at the gunmetal sky and at the people huddling against the wind. He felt sick to the pit of his stomach.

Ray Sussock walked into the incident room. Donoghue saw him and smiled.

'Ray,' he said, taking his pipe from his mouth. 'I thought you'd be resting. I take it you didn't turn anything else up yesterday?'

'No; I finished late and had a lie-in this morning, sir, then I got bored. It's all very well having a day off, but you have to do something with it. I haven't anything to do, so I came in.'

'Glad to see you. I needed the company. No offence, laddie,' he said to the nearby PC.

'None taken, sir,' said the duty constable.

'Anything happening, sir?'

'Not a thing. It's all very quiet, maybe too quiet.'

'You think he's going to strike again tonight?'

'I don't know, Ray. He's been quiet for one night and

we haven't had another tape. You never know with head-bangers, and this one moves very quickly, one a night, almost, and so if he lays off for one night it's a calm before the storm.'

'Aye; who's on, sir?'

'Montgomerie's having a pleasant time reliving his student days, but he hasn't turned anything up. King's picked up a missing person, a boy. I didn't like it, I think he's got enough on with this Slow Tom character, but short of asking him to knock on every door in the city in the hope of finding someone with Slow Tom written on his forehead there was nothing I could give him. Anyway, he seemed eager enough, so . . .' Donoghue spread an up-turned palm.

'He's still got a good half-dozen open cases on his case-load, he could have attended to those. He hasn't room for any more.'

'None of us has room for any more. Let's go to my office. I could use a gallon of coffee. Have you eaten yet?'

Sussock said he had. Donoghue ordered coffee. It was brought up and he and Sussock sat on either side of the desk with the stainless steel pot between them.

'Are you worried about it, sir?' asked Sussock, sipping his coffee.

'The case? Yes I'm worried about it. I couldn't rest at home; I'd snap at my family.'

'I feel we're not getting anywhere, we don't know a thing about this guy. Are you getting any flak from Findlater?'

'Not yet, I see him every day and tell him what we've done, which is a lot, and then I tell him what we've found out, which is very little. In fact, all we've got so far is one angry young man facing a charge of wasting police time, from which he'll probably be acquitted. He doesn't seem un-duly bothered — Findlater, that is — and that worries me.'

'How?'

'Well, I'd be happier if he was pressing me for results and threatening to take charge of the investigation.' Donoghue leaned forward and grabbed the coffee pot and replenished his cup. 'But he's not. Every afternoon I knock on his door and wait to be asked in and then I give him a progress report which usually consists of two sentences, and he says "O.K., carry on." ' He raised his cup to his lips. 'Ray, I think he's waiting until I tell him we're within an ace of an arrest and then he'll assume command.'

'I wouldn't put it past him. He's a fly bastard.'

'Puts me in a difficult position. Tell me, Ray, shall I deliberately withhold information and see this thing to its conclusion, or shall I keep him fully informed and so let him come in at the kill and take a lot of credit for doing nothing?'

'Don't know, sir, you have to keep him informed, I suppose, but in the services orders and messages were known to go astray from time to time. Anyway, let's catch the bugger first, then we'll talk about that one.'

'You're right, I'm a premature worrier. Although you're wrong when you say we don't know anything about him. We know he's a first-generation graduate or someone who's made a class change, he's immature and he's a natural guitarist and he probably comes from the Dumbarton/Helensburgh area. But not further west because he doesn't roll his r's enough.'

'Do what?'

'His r's, Ray.' Donoghue smiled to himself. 'He doesn't roll them enough.'

'Oh,' said Sussock.

'So said Sam Payne.' Donoghue grinned.

'Was he the . . . ?'

'. . . Thug in the leather jacket who sat at my desk yesterday? Yes that was him. The lad's got a head on his shoulders. I've phoned round the colleges and the universities to ask them to check their rolls for male students from the north bank, but none of the registrars would release the information. I suppose they're right to do that, but it doesn't make our job any easier.' Donoghue's phone rang. He picked it up and Sussock saw his eyebrows rise slightly as he listened. 'Ask him to come up,' said Donoghue, and replaced the receiver.

'Visitor?' asked Sussock, but Donoghue didn't reply. The two men sat in silence, sipping at their coffee. There was a knock at the door and a constable showed Sam Payne into the room. He was wearing the same leather jacket, but Donoghue noticed that the look of energetic and youthful confidence had gone.

'Come in, Sam.' Donoghue stood and smiled. 'Coffee?'

Sussock also stood and smiled at the young man.

'No thank you, sir.'

'What can we do for you, Sam? Please sit down.'

'Well, it's about the tape, sir,' said Sam Payne, sitting nervously. 'I was thinking about it last night. I'm trespassing on your territory, I know, tell me to shove off if you want.'

Donoghue sat down. 'Carry on, Sam.'

'Well, I've been reading the newspapers and it struck me that there's nothing on the tape that isn't in the papers. Have you considered the possibility that the tape is a hoax? It would fit with the immaturity of the person who made it.'

Donoghue bowed his head and looked at the files on his desk, and the coffee pot and at his pipe and gold-plated lighter. It was his way of apologizing for being a fool.

Sussock said, 'I'm going to nail that bastard.' After a minute Sam Payne left the room, quietly shutting the door behind him.

The Rock was an up-market version of The Auld Hoose. The Rock was a grey, squat bar, a concrete complex, a centrally heated, wall-to-wall (red tartan) carpeted pill-box. It was up-market because it had windows and was set back from Highburgh Road, G12. There were low beams on the ceiling, wooden chairs and tables, a television perched in the corner, and a recess near the toilets for the pool table. There was a hat-and-coat-rack in the corner, and a long gantry, behind which were the barmen, who all wore blue shirts and baggy trousers. The bar was beginning to fill with Saturday night youth, and the juke box, which offered one hundred and twenty selections, seemed to be playing the same five records over and over again. At the door a man in a blazer and peaked cap checked the identification of suspiciously under-age-looking girls. Montgomerie sat in a large circle of people crowded round three tables underneath the window, a trifle too near the juke box, but seats anywhere in the Rock on a Saturday night are a priceless commodity. His left hand rested on Gillian's leg. Gillian had proved to be quite a catch: attracted to her because of her pert bottom clasped in denim, he had subsequently found that she (a) went like the Glasgow-Edinburgh express and (b) knew a lot of people who played guitars, who knew other people who played guitars, etc, etc. Gillian, for her part, had been without a man since the beginning of the academic year and was now pleased to have a bearded one sitting with his hand on her knee, especially since he happened to be tall, good-looking, worldly-wise, and seemed to have more money than any other post-grad she had met. She looked warm, her cheeks were full, her eyes were wide and she couldn't help smiling. Montgomerie's eyes and ears missed nothing, but he said little; his mouth was mostly used for drinking Belhaven with relish.

He scanned the room. Most of the clientele were young, a lot were very young, young enough for Montgomerie to feel old—and, were it not for Gillian's flesh, out of it, over the hill, past it. He wondered if he was getting to that point in life when you are nearer the end than the beginning. He was only twenty-six but it was old enough for the other people in the bar to look like children, velvet-smooth chins and giggling nervousness, and they were drinking hard, three deep at the bar, knocking it back like steel-makers and clamouring for more. He wondered was he like this at university, a child thinking he was a man because he had pubic hair and a glass of amber-coloured liquid in his hand? Going to change the world, but not on a Saturday night because that was the night grants were used to keep the breweries solvent?

Sometimes, Montgomerie thought, sometimes it isn't comfortable to see yourself.

A man walked into the bar. He was in his fifties, balding, portly; he had a dripping Burberry and a battered trilby. A lot of young faces turned and glanced at him, probably because he stuck out like a white rhino at a tea party. The man seemed to be looking for somebody and Montgomerie wondered how he could attract his attention. The man was Ray Sussock.

Montgomerie moved his arm and scratched his head. the man saw the movement, nodded towards Montgomerie and walked towards the toilets. Montgomerie patted Gillian on the knee and stood.

'He's burst at last,' said a boy who was hiding his youth behind a ginger beard. The group laughed and Montgomerie smiled.

'Don't go away,' he said.

He and Sussock stood side by side at the urinals. Behind them, inside the cubicle, somebody was smoking cannabis.

'You'll get a bust there,' hissed Sussock.

'He'll still be in his nappies.'

'Any progress?'

'No. Not a dicky-bird. I needed this piss, I never know when to go in case I miss something. How did you know where to find me?'

'You gave your movements to Fabian this morning when you telephoned in.'

'Did I? Oh, yeah . . . yeah, I did.' Montgomerie had said he'd be in the Rock that evening because Donoghue had insisted on a place for each phase of the day. But it was only six to four odds-on that Gillian and her gang would opt for the Rock.

'Losing your memory, Constable? Don't let the good life get to you.'

'Oh I'm not, Sarge, I'm not,' Montgomerie whispered earnestly.

'That's good, because we're taking you off the case.'

'C'mon!' Montgomerie turned to him. 'It's hardly my fault I haven't heard anything. Anyway, I'm in with an interesting bunch, they're into guitars and folk music. I hope to get a lead.'

'I noticed. Who is the girl?'

'Just a girl. Part of the interesting bunch.'

'Anyway, stick with it,' Sussock said.

'I thought you said you were taking me off the case?'

'We are. You're now looking for a hoaxer.'

'J.C.'

'Right. Fabian wants him badly. He's screwed up the whole investigation.'

'What do you know about him?'

'We don't know the colour of his hair, that's for sure. Or his blood group, but it may be "O".'

'Just the voice, then?'

'Aye. Can you remember it?'

'Aye.'

'Fabian had a couple of university teachers in, one was wearing a leather jacket. I'm getting old.'

'I know how you feel.'

'Anyway, he's thought to be immature. That should make us both feel older, first nail in the coffin.'

'They're all immature.'

'This one was even more so. He comes from Dumbarton way. Working-class parents and he's a good guitar player. That's your best line. Apparently he's a natural.'

'O.K.' said Montgomerie, flicking his penis at the urinal. 'A guitar player, working-class origins, from Dumbarton.'

'No further west. He doesn't roll his r's enough.'

'Do what?'

'Roll his r's, Montgomerie, his r's.'

'Oh.'

'Just don't get too comfortable, we're still likely to pull you out at any time.' Sussock pulled up his zip.

'O.K., O.K.'

They rinsed their hands and separately left the toilets. Montgomerie went back to his place in the group, to his seat by the radiator, to his beer and his girl. Ray Sussock went back into the snow.

In Edinburgh a mother and her daughter were baking in the kitchen. The mother was thirty-five years old, she was a handsome woman with sharp features and short hair and a slim figure. Her daughter was ten and kneaded her piece of dough just like her mother was kneading her larger piece. In the front room a boy was playing with toy soldiers on the carpet in front of the fire. He was eight years old and knocked the soldiers down by skimming a domino at them. The domino was a shell fired from a Tiger tank and was killing the Tommies who were trying to destroy it. Of the Tommies left standing the boy had already identified the one who would rush forward and heroically save his comrades. The boy was getting tired but he had been allowed to stay up late and so he fought the sleepiness. He tossed the domino again and more soldiers died.

'It's gym on Monday,' said the girl to her mother. 'I

don't mind it, but it's so cold, we have to run across the yard to the gym.'

'But that doesn't take very long, dear,' replied the woman warmly, but firmly. 'A matter of seconds.' The woman had seen the school buildings on open days and knew that the gym was a new building about fifty yards from the main schoolhouse. The children had to walk or, in the rain, run, along a tarmac path in order to get from one building to another. She was quite pleased that her daughter had to endure this small hardship; she felt that because of it, and other similar experiences, her daughter would find her adult life easier to cope with.

'But I get so cold, Mummy.'

'You can use your overcoat, can't you?'

'Yes, but my legs get cold.'

'Well, we shall have to hope it's thawing on Monday. Come on, this is ready for the oven.'

The family heard car tyres on the gravel drive which had been cleared of snow and they ran to welcome the man as he opened the front door. His children hugged a leg each and his wife put a powdery arm around his neck and kissed him.

Fabian Donoghue had come home.

Whether Sunday ever dawned was a moot point. Certainly there was a time when the street lights were switched off, and a time when the stars could no longer be seen, a time about 9.30 a.m. when the darkness gave way to a grey half-light, a chilling and an empty greyness which covered Glasgow like a wet army blanket and which would give way to nothing until the darkness came again at 4 p.m.

It was Sunday morning in Glasgow, the city was still and quiet, on the seventh day its citizens rested in the struggle against the winter, save perhaps for a solitary venture over the ice to collect the Sunday papers. Sunday morning in the working city, and, like every other city and town in the British Isles the adult population were either nursing hangovers or preparing for worship. At 10.30 Malcolm Montgomerie's throat felt like the bottom of a budgie's cage and his headache had moved to a concentrated attack on two square inches of skull just above his left ear. At the side of him Gillian was being sick into a plastic bucket. At 10.30 Richard and Rosemary King took their children to Meeting for Worship at the Friends' Meeting House.

Richard King was not a Quaker, he was not even a Christian. But he had married a girl from a Quaker family who now sat next to him in Meeting with her head bowed and her hands crossed on her lap and who would call herself by the endearing and archaic term 'Quakeress'. He admired and respected the Society of Friends for their grasp of an ideology he felt himself not yet ready to grasp and he respected them for the girl they had raised to a woman for him to marry, and he felt he would like to do the same for his children.

He hoped that by the time his children were old enough to challenge him on his beliefs he would have assumed some Christian commitment and so be able to defend his actions of today, but at the moment he was giving them something and that, he felt, was the important thing.

The children sat in the first fifteen minutes of the meeting and then an adult stood and opened a side door. Without a word being spoken the children slipped off the benches and padded out of the room. They were going to Sunday School in a downstairs room and would file back five minutes before the handshaking which signified the close of the meeting. Last Sunday the children did the United Nations. He watched his children go; he felt proud and at the same time terrified of parenthood.

About him most heads were bowed. One man beamed at the ceiling and another stared out of the window.

King felt clumsy amongst the gentle, vain amongst the humble, and thoughtless among the pensive. Everybody around him seemed to know what they were doing. From the next building came a dull knocking sound. It was not at all disturbing and seemed to contribute strangely to the silence.

He thought if he was a Christian he ought to be praying. Who for? His family? That would be selfish. Who, then? The murderer, the man who is stabbing people in the cold and snow-bound city? For Donoghue and his loneliness of command? But he wasn't a Christian, he did not believe.

He wondered what his children were doing. Somebody shifted on the bench. Somebody else coughed.

He felt guilty that he couldn't follow a train of thought, or ponder upon an issue. He wanted to reach for the Bible which lay on the shelf which ran along the back of the bench in front of him, because at least it would give him something to read, but he hesitated in case by moving he would show his wife that he was restless.

He decided that if he was a Christian he would pray for the McAlpine family of Partick. A good policeman can switch off, he can leave his work at his desk, but not all policemen can switch off all the time and every policeman has one case, at least one, that pursues him in his free time, that makes him depressed in the bar at night, that upsets him during fitful sleep and haunts his innermost thoughts. Richard King knew that if he was a Christian his prayers would be with the McAlpines of Partick.

In front of him a woman stood and cleared her throat. The Meeting stirred, people shifted on the benches, raising their heads. The woman said that the knocking from the next building reminded her that Christ was ever knocking at our hearts and it was our duty to let him in. Then she sat down. Heads bowed, ruminating on the woman's words, and the banging took on a new significance.

King knew that throughout his life he would never forget the visit he had made to the McAlpines. The little girl running into her bedroom.

The banging began to sound metallic and hollow. A central heating system being installed? On a Sunday? The black economy, nudge, wink, the old man would charge three ton for this but me and the boys will do it for half-price on Sunday, cash.

He remembered the kitchen door needed painting.

Very suddenly he knew that the McAlpine boy was dead. All along, even from the moment he had picked up the file and put it on his desk, he would have been surprised if the boy had turned up alive. But for the first time he now *knew* he was dead. He didn't know how he knew, he just knew. He was as certain that the McAlpine boy was dead as he was certain that that night he would make love to the beautiful Quakeress who sat head bowed beside him. It was a similar kind of certainty, and he was certain of what he knew.

He also knew that Jamie McPherson, who lived in Partick with his father, who had run from the police one morning in Riverside, who had a ring in his ear and a boyish face and who had been in Paisley police cells when the first murder had taken place, had killed the McAlpine boy. King had released him from questioning on the Monday and he had killed on the Thursday.

He told himself he mustn't blame himself. He told himself he must never tell his wife, but he knew he would tell her that night in bed, long afterwards, while they were just lying there silently.

He wondered if he could arrest somebody for murder if he had no body.

He wondered if he should be thinking such things in a Meeting for Worship.

He wondered when his children were coming back. He
wanted to look at his watch but he didn't want to show his
wife that he was restless.

I don't know when I'll be back. Yes, I've got to go out.
No, it's not the bird, the bird's all right. You don't
have to throw it out. You mustn't. I know it's late, stop
nagging at me.

It's still cold. I wonder when the summer's coming?
When it's like this I think the summer will never come.
I think the winter's dug in, it's got hold of the earth
and it's not going to let go. Down on the coast on an
outing, I once saw a crab's leg and the pincers had
round a bit of driftwood. The crab was gone, but the
leg was still there with the pincers still holding the piece
of wood. Winter's like that, winter's a big white claw.

Tonight's going to be dangerous, I went yesterday
and I went the day before. Just to check it out.

It's cold.

I'll take the bus. A 56 across the city. It's not going to
be easy. It's going to be the first one I know. She
doesn't know me, but I know her. I saw her from the
Welfare minibus. Three months ago on our way back
from the Transport Museum. She got out of the car
and went into her house. Rich bitch, big house.

She needs learning.

Lissu told me. He told me about her and he told me
that tonight's the night. Three days ago he told me it
was to be her.

I'll come back and finish the book. I don't need
much sleep.

I read a lot.

CHAPTER 8

She was twenty-six years old, five-ten and weighing ten stones, she had shoulder-length blonde hair, blue eyes and high cheekbones, but not too high, and she had a small mouth, but not too small. She was wearing a black evening gown from Pepperoni and her full-length fur coat was a Cooney; she wore a Cartier watch on her left wrist and a bracelet from Baume and Mercier on the other. Her sheer tights were from Bloomingdales and her boots were from Midas. Her handbag was an Etienne Aigner, and inside was her driving licence and car keys. The name on the licence was Susan Smith and the keys fitted a shiny Morgan plus-8 tourer which was parked in the driveway of her house. Susan Smith had an alias, a pseudonym, a trade name, it was 'Simone', and Simone had been in the first division of the London modelling circuit until she came north to become Scotland's No. 1 model. She bought a house on Albert Drive which had previously been owned by a whisky baron and had had it completely redecorated while she was holidaying at Champneys. She was now lying on the sixteen foot long sofa with one delicate foot resting on the pile of the Durri carpet. She was staring at the ceiling. She was cold. She was dead.

Donoghue stared down at the body. She had been stabbed twice, once in her throat, and a small hand with perfectly manicured fingernails was resting on a bloody gash in her evening gown, just over her stomach. He was mesmerized by the body. He felt that all deaths which warrant a police investigation have an element of sadness, murders more than others, and the murder of the young and the beautiful have the most sadness of all.

A camera bulb flashed and Donoghue was brought sharply back to reality. Ray Sussock was standing by his side, Jimmy Bothwell dusted the hi-fi for fingerprints, two photographers recorded the body and aspects of the room. The ambulance crew waited until they were given permission to remove the body. There were voices from the next room where Richard King was talking to Ellen Murphy. The camera bulb flashed again.

'No doubt about who did this, sir?' said Sussock.

'You know, Ray, I almost wish that the tape wasn't a hoax,' Donoghue mused. 'At least then we'd know he's only got four more to go after this. Ray, this is five murders committed by the same man in nine days and we don't know a single solitary thing about him, Ray, not one lousy thing to set him apart from all the other guys in Glasgow who have light-coloured hair and wear donkey jackets. We're going to find the same thing under her fingernails; see, one of them has been split; she put up a struggle, that coffee table is over, and that poker's away from its fitting, but we are going to be just as much in the dark as we were nine days ago. Forensic will tell us the attacker was male with light-coloured hair and that his blood group is AB-negative.'

'He must have been big to overpower her,' said Ray Sussock. 'That's a new indication. I mean, she's not a small lassie, and it looks like she had the poker to defend herself.'

'Probably. I wouldn't put money on it. No sign of forced entry,' Donoghue glanced at the windows, 'she probably knew him.'

'That's what we thought about Margaret Stewart. It didn't get us very far. Either he knew her or he's got a neat way of getting into people's houses and enticing secretaries on to building sites. The attack in people's homes is a new one. It's bloody frightening; who is this guy, Ray?'

Ray Sussock shook his head. The dead girl reminded him of Elka Willems. What if she had been knifed? He felt sick. Who was this guy?

'Who found her, Ray, the cleaner, you say?'

'Aye,' Sussock nodded. There was a faraway sound in his voice.

Ellen Murphy was forty-five. She had a red scarf round her head and wore a patterned blue smock and blue slacks. She had tried to drink a cup of sweetened tea which King had made her, but she couldn't lift it to her lips because her hands were shaking too much. She settled for a Three Fives cigarette and King struck the match for her.

'I'm sorry; it must be hard for you, Mrs Murphy; but you say you came in and found her on the settee?'

The woman nodded. 'Oh, the poor wee lassie, she was so young and attractive.'

'You have a key to the house, Mrs Murphy?'

'Aye.' She pulled on the cigarette and took the smoke deep into her lungs. 'I cleaned for old Mr Balfour before he died . . . Miss Smith kept me on. She even paid a retainer while the house was being done.'

'Do you come in every day?'

'Three mornings a week. Sometimes she'd ask me to do a day if she was going to have a party and I'd also do a day after the party. She had plenty of friends. The men swarmed round her, but I don't think she had a regular man-friend. Sometimes when I called in the morning there would be another car in the driveway and I'd never go upstairs then, but I never saw the same car twice. I think she was a lonely girl, sir.'

'Sir.' King winced.

'What time did you arrive this morning, Mrs Murphy?'

'Eight; no, a bit later. Quarter past eight, sir. Around that time.'

'There was nothing outside the house to make you

think something was wrong?'

'No, I was the first person to walk up the drive since the snow had stopped falling. I let myself in and saw Miss Smith lying there. I don't remember much after that. I'm sorry, sir.'

When the police had arrived they had found Mrs Murphy sitting on the stairs with the telephone receiver still in her hand.

'O.K., love,' said King, and patted her hand. 'We're going to take you to the hospital now. This lady is going to drive you there.'

'No, my work! Monday's the day I do downstairs, it gets filthy over the weekend. I can't go yet.'

'I want you to go, hen,' said King.

'You want me to go, sir?'

King nodded and smiled.

'If you want me to go then, sir . . .'

King nodded to Elka Willems, who took Mrs Murphy by the arm and gently guided her down the trampled snow of the driveway to where an unmarked car waited.

In the drawing-room the photographer handed a bundle of Polaroid prints to Donoghue and then turned to help his assistant to pack their gear away. 'The rest will be on your desk in two hours, sir,' said the photographer.

'Fine,' Donoghue grunted. He looked at the photographs and reflected that they would be the last photographs ever taken of the legendary Simone, alias Susan Smith, late of Beeston, Notts. Turning to Bothwell he said, 'Anything?'

Bothwell stood by the fireplace, short-cropped ginger hair, National Health spectacles; he looked to Donoghue more like an awkward fifth-former than a forensic chemist. 'Quite a lot, sir,' he stammered. 'Well, about six sets so far, I think, but one will be hers, though.'

'Evidently,' said Sussock.

Donoghue just sighed. 'Carry on,' he said, and, turning

to Sussock, 'Let's take a sniff upstairs, Ray.'

To Donoghue's taste the bedroom was too big and the
ceiling was too high; it was anything but a cosy, homely
room. Donoghue would get lost in this bedroom. The
wardrobes were set in the wall and the carpet was a vast
expanse of deep white pile, the bottom of the curtains lay
on the floor two feet away from the wall, and the bed
itself was a large oval piece of furniture with lace awnings
and lemon-coloured silk duvet and sheet. There was a
lemon-coloured dressing table set in the recess between
two wardrobes and on the mirror, written in lipstick in a
small, almost unintelligible hand, was THIS IS FOR LISSU.

'Better get Bothwell up here,' said Donoghue. 'And the
photographers before they go.'

Sussock turned to go downstairs.

'Where do you think she kept her address book, Ray?'
Ray Sussock left the bedroom. He already felt tired.

The address book was tracked down in the kitchen.
Richard King found it and noticed that the kitchen seemed
to be the only part of the house which reflected life, which
seemed to have been lived in, it was the only room where
there was something unwashed, where there was something waiting to be attended to. It seemed to King to be
the only place in the house where Simone could be Susan
Smith, free of her role, free to be herself. The address
book was an exercise book with a snoopy sticker on the
front and it was found in the drawer which contained the
carving knives.

King took the address book to Donoghue, who cross-
referred it with her diary which was kept on the telephone
table in the hall. According to the diary she had spent the
previous night with Jeremy, who had picked her up at 8
for dinner. There was only one Jeremy in the address
book, his last name was Alexander and he had an address
in G12. 'On your way, Ray,' said Donoghue.

Donoghue looked back over Susan Smith's last month

of life. It had mostly consisted of what she had referred to as 'engagement (studio)' or 'engagement (location)', though he was at a loss as to what possible locations could be offered by the west of Scotland in the grip of winter, unless she was modelling Arctic survival gear, which doubtless would show the sex appeal in her eyes. Her evenings had mostly been spent being taken out to dinner by 'Ron' or 'James' or 'Hamish' or 'Iain', all of whom would be found in her address book and interviewed. He looked forward. The entry for that day, January 25th, read:

   10.00 — pick up air tickets.
  Afternoon — pack. Inform police, leave Mrs Murphy's
    money.
   7.30 — Flight from Abbotsinch.

 The days of the next two weeks had been scored out; at the top of each page she had written 'Morocco Engagement'. In the address book Donoghue came across the entry 'Mum and Dad' and took a note of the address against it.

Jeremy Alexander was a photographer who had rooms on Great Western Road, east of the Byres Road intersection. His 'rooms' were large and there were a lot of them; Sussock wasn't sure, but he reckoned about eight in all. One door had DARK ROOM printed on it, another seemed to be a store room for equipment, a third an office. One was a studio. Sussock hadn't been in a studio before, but he knew that Jeremy Alexander was a photographer and so he presumed that the room with the black Japanese cameras on tripods, with the table top arranged with lenses, with the battery of lights, with odd bits of furniture, like a hammock, and assorted plants like palms in a row against the wall, was in fact a studio.

 Jeremy Alexander was the sort of man who, if he chose not to look through a lense and press the shutter button, could have made an equally successful career on the other side of the camera. He was tall and slim, he had a smooth and balanced face which was pleasing to the eye in the way in which a woman's face is pleasing. He seemed to know it, and Sussock detected a badly suppressed smile and a faint look of contempt as Jeremy Alexander swung the door wide on the policeman. It served to make Sussock feel even more old, overweight and bedraggled. He couldn't even give Alexander a hard time, because the photographer's hair was black.

The photographer inspected Sussock's ID in a leisurely manner and then beckoned him into the flat. He walked ahead of Sussock and led him into the studio. As they entered the room a red-haired girl glided past them. She walked with her heels raised, evidently used to walking with something under them, even if it was only centrally heated air. She didn't look at Sussock. She was wearing a white towelling robe: Sussock knew there was nothing underneath.

'Five minutes, darling,' said Jeremy Alexander. He was wearing a red T-shirt and had a light-meter slung around his neck. The heating in the flat was turned up high, the lights in the studio made it even hotter, and Sussock was draped in damp clothes; he felt the weight on his shoulders and the beads of sweat begin to run off his brow and down his spine. In a few moments he would be stepping back out into the winter. He knew he was in for a cold.

'So what can I do for you?' said the photographer in a tone which let Sussock know he was being done a big favour. Jeremy Alexander slipped his slim hips on to the table and lit a Fribourg and Treyer.

'It concerns a lady called Susan Smith,' said Sussock icily. 'I believe you know her?'

'Do I?' He blew a thin plume of smoke which didn't quite reach Sussock's face. 'Susan Smith? The name isn't familiar, officer, though I may have her on my books.'

'You may know her as Simone?'

'Oh, Simone, of course I know Simone. I'm expecting her some time today. In fact, when you rang the door bell I expected to find her delectable form. I can't say that you're a good swap, Mr Sissock.'

'Sussock.'

'Oh,' said Jeremy Alexander.

'When did you see her last?'

'Why?'

'Just answer the question, please.'

Alexander shrugged his left shoulder. 'Last night. We had dinner. It was a celebration.'

'Celebration?'

'Of our first contract. Morocco, don't you know?'

'No, I don't. Tell me.'

'She gave her last agent the boot,' said Alexander with forced patience. 'He tried to hold her to their contract but she sat in front of the camera with her tongue out. He got the message. I met her in a London night club and she said she reckoned she was good enough, but she wasn't getting to the top. I mean *the* top. I told her about the new North and said she could carve Scotland up. Nothing, but nothing, could touch her. We signed a contract, I got a straight ten per cent. We did a lot of modelling work, and we shot her nude, it's good enough for the top-flight glossies. She stands to net eighty thousand pounds, that's eight Gs for me. Few weeks ago I worked her first international contract with Emile Celave. You know him?'

Sussock confessed he didn't know Emile Celave, nor had Sussock heard of him in any context whatsoever.

'Mmm,' said Alexander. 'Well, he's one of the best. He was shooting her in the coming season's beachwear in Morocco.'

'Cold, this time of year.'

'Simone stands to get a few goose-bumps but the sea is blue and the sky is bluer, even in January. It looks O.K. on celluloid. You've also got the advantage of deserted beaches. Even better on celluloid.'

'Did you take her home?'

'Last night? Uh-huh. We had dinner to celebrate her going away and then I took her home. We ate at Fabrizio's. Why?'

'Because she's dead.'

The man's jaw dropped. He gripped the table top with both hands. The cigarette smouldered away in his right hand. He said, 'The silly cow.'

'You don't seem too upset.'

'Upset! Christ, man you don't know how upset I am. What about my contract? Dead . . .'

'Tell me about taking her home.'

'Sod that, what am I going to do? She was my future.'

'When did you arrive at her house?'

'Why is that important? I haven't got anything to replace her. I mean anything.' His voice dropped to a whisper. 'That female there, she's the nearest I've got and she hasn't got the right proportions. She'll turn heads in Sauchiehall Street but she doesn't have what it takes to be in front of a camera. We're doing a composition for a down-market men's mag and she's getting a reduced payment 'cos I strung her along and said it was her entry into the big time. That's the level I'm down to.'

'What time?' There was an edge to Sussock's voice.

'What time? Who cares what time?'

'I care what time.'

'I can't even sell her nude slides—they won't print posthumously. Did you know that? I could have made eight, maybe ten thousand.'

'Alexander, we could do this the hard way.'

'I could sell down-market . . .'

'Christ's sake!'

'O.K., O.K.'

'What time did you take her home?'

'Early, why?'

'Because she was killed just after she entered her house. What time would that have been?'

'Ten-thirty. Bit later, probably. Early, anyway. She had to be up in the morning. What shall I do now, take wedding photographs?'

'That's your problem. Did you go in with her?'

'Just inside.'

'Did you see anybody?'

'No. I followed her in after she bent down and opened the door.'

'She bent down?'

'She had a lovely bum. Even under a fur coat she had a lovely bum. Her key was under the mat.'

'Under the mat!'

'Would hardly credit it, would you? And she had to dig it out.'

'She kept the key under the mat?'

'In front of the door, under the snow was a mat. Under the mat was a key. The key fitted the lock of the door.'

'Was the snow disturbed when you reached the door?'

'Yes.'

'Did you reach the door together?'

'No. I had to negotiate a snowdrift. The car . . . anyway, when I got to the door she was already in the house. That's why the snow was disturbed when I got there.'

'Was the snow disturbed when she got there?'

'Can't say.'

'How long did you stay with her?'

'Couple of minutes.'

'Go anywhere in the house?'

'Hall. Through to the kitchen. Noticed she seemed to like the kitchen. Funny, you'd think she'd want to get away from all that domesticity thing.'

'And you didn't see anything?'

'I told you once.'

'You didn't hear anything as you were walking away?'

'No.'

'She was fully dressed, outdoor clothes I mean, when she was killed. She couldn't have been in the house more than a couple of minutes before she was attacked, and we think she put up a struggle. You certain you didn't see or hear anything?'

'Like I said, man. Listen, what about my future? I had the big time in my hands . . . Who did it?'

'The head-banger.'

'Slow Tom?'

'Well, you could say that.'

'What do you mean by that?'

'You'll find out soon enough.'

'Who is this guy?'

'If we knew that we wouldn't be here stopping your re-entry into the glittering world of showbiz. Think back, Alexander.'

'I'm thinking.'

'Hard!'

'Listen. I parked the car and walked up her driveway.'

'How many sets of footprints in the snow leading to her door?'

'One. Hers. It was snowing hard. By the time she had reached the door the prints she had made on the roadside had disappeared. I've never seen snow like it.' He drew on his cigarette. Sussock noticed his hand was shaking. 'Anyway, I followed her in; I hardly saw anything, my head was down against the snow. I went into the house, through to the kitchen where she was. I stayed for two minutes. I pecked her on the cheek once, you know, we had a strictly professional relationship. She said thanks for the evening and what time should she bring her car round? I was going to look after her car for the fortnight, get it serviced, you know. So I said it was my pleasure and any time after ten-thirty. Then I left and pulled the door shut behind me. I saw and heard nothing unusual. The mat was standing against the wall. I put it back and went into the snow.'

'The mat?'

'She kept the key under it. I told you.'

'Yes, yes,' said Sussock to himself. 'That explains how he got in.'

'Good. That's your problem solved. So what about mine?'

'Call round Sunday, we'll see what we can find in the poor-box.'

On the stairs Sussock felt the sweat on his brow and between his shoulderblades begin to freeze. By the time he reached the close mouth he could feel the first trace of shivering. On the street he joined the line of people walking near the walls. The other line was walking near the gutter. The day had brought a watery sun and the sun was causing a thaw. During the morning snow slipped off the roofs and crashed sixty feet to the ground to lie in a long moraine down the centre of the pavement. Sussock walked between the long mound of snow and the shop fronts; he was shivering and his legs began to feel weak.

At 10.30 a.m. Malcolm Montgomerie was loping down Byres Road with a copy of the *Daily Record* under his arm. He had just been in telephone contact with Donoghue who had told him about Susan Smith, alias Simone. He had recovered from his Sunday morning hangover (which had lasted well into Sunday afternoon) and he could now look at the Rubáiyát without feeling sick. He would be out for a bevvy the night, but right then he suddenly had things to do. Right then he was acting on suspicion.

Right then there was a man walking in front of him. The man was wearing a kaftan, he had long golden hair and was carrying a guitar. Montgomerie pulled his collar up against the cold and plunged his hands deeper into his jacket pockets and increased his pace until he was twenty feet behind the man, then slowed and matched the man's pace. The man had a slow, casual walk, his head was high and he seemed to be savouring the air. Some air to savour, wispy snow and windblown drops of melting ice. His kaftan wasn't any cheap imitation, it was heavy and thick and swayed gently from side to side as he walked. He went into the University Café. Montgomerie waited in case the man was only buying cigarettes, but when he didn't reappear Montgomerie too entered the café.

The University Café smacked of the 1930s; thin benches, jutting from the walls, heavy stained wood panelling. An Espresso coffee machine wheezed near the till. It had a strange atmosphere, to Montgomerie it was the 1930s but 1930s Paris or 1930s New York, he couldn't decide. The café was almost deserted; three taxi drivers sat in the corner with their plastic money-holders on the table in front of them. An old lady in ragged clothes mumbled to herself. The man in the kaftan sat alone at a bench with his back to a partition and his left arm leaning against the wall, just under a certificate of merit somebody had achieved for ice-cream making. Montgomerie sat adjacent to him.

The man looked like Jesus Christ. His long blonde hair was centrally parted, he had a beard and moustache, both untrimmed. He looked at Montgomerie and smiled with glazed blue eyes. Montgomerie was reminded of the time some years previously when he had been in a room in a flat near the Meadows in Edinburgh. It was a darkened room, the air was full of the soft sweet smell of cannabis and Indian music was coming out of the hi-fi speakers. Montgomerie had long hair then and his moccasins had come all the way from *Exchange and Mart*. The other person in the room was another man who also looked like Jesus Christ. He had had a small monkey which he kept as a pet; it was attached to the man's trouser belt with a thin chain. Suddenly the man picked up his banjo and began to hit the monkey over the head. The room was filled with squeals and hollow resonance and he didn't stop until the monkey was dead. Montgomerie had stopped relating the story when he found that people just laughed, it may have sounded funny, but Montgomerie didn't think it was. It wasn't funny at the time and years later when he understood about breakdowns it still wasn't funny. Since then he could never bring himself to trust young men who looked like Jesus Christ.

The waitress was an Italian-looking woman with a dour expression. Montgomerie said he'd take an Espresso. He thought he shouldn't have sat so near the man; he thought he should have tailed him; he couldn't believe his own stupidity. He'd given the game away. So what did he do now, drink the coffee and go back outside and wait for the guy to come out and hope he didn't recognize him, and then continue to follow him? Or say, 'Excuse me, sir, I am a police officer and I observed you travelling along Byres Road in a southerly direction with a guitar in your hand . . .' to which the man would reply, 'Yes?' In the end Montgomerie forced a smile and asked Jesus of Nazareth if he played that thing.

'I was wondering when you were going to say something, Officer,' said the man, continuing to smile with his eyes.

'What made you say that?' Montgomerie wasn't feeling too clever.

'Because you are a polis man,' said the man in the kaftan, 'are you not?'

'What makes you think that?' said Montgomerie.

'Only a polis person would say that. You've clinched it,

polis person.' The man smiled. 'But if you want to know the truth . . .'

'I want to know the truth.'

'Don't cut me off in mid-sentence, polis person. If you want to know the truth, only a person of homosexual leaning or a polis would sit opposite me when over half the seats in the café are empty. I don't think you have a doubtful hormonal balance and so I think you are a polis person. Also you followed me down the road but waited for a few minutes before following me in here. Was it to see if I was just popping in to get some nails?'

'O.K. How did you know I was following you down the road?'

'I could see your reflection in the glass in the shop door-ways, polis man. A bit like wing-mirrors on a car, they are. You walked rapidly, running almost until you were a few paces behind me.'

'Not unobservant, are you?'

'I was also expecting you, polis man.'

'Why?'

'I read the news.' He tapped Montgomerie's newspaper. 'Slow Tom is a male and has blond hair.'

'Light-coloured. Got an alibi, have you?' Montgomerie was no longer solely interested in men with light hair, but he played out the part.

'Och aye.' The man sipped his coffee and took a bite of his hamburger. The waitress brought Montgomeries's coffee.

'Tell me. Last night, for instance?' The telephone con-versation he had had with Donoghue just before sighting the man was still fresh in his mind. He seemed to feel the death of Simone more than the other deaths. He had once seen her picture.

'Last night, no alibi. Mind you, when the old bird was killed a couple of nights ago I was playing in a club. Witnesses to the power n, where n is large and positive. I also can't be fitted up because I can't play twelve-bar blues. It said in the paper the murderer plays good twelve-bar blues.'

'You can't?'

'No.'

'Perhaps you could point us in the right direction?'

'Perhaps I could.'

Montgomerie's eyes narrowed.

'Cost you,' said the man, pushing the remainder of his hamburger into his mouth. Montgomerie noticed a gold filling.

'What?' he said.

'Buy me breakfast, oh polis person. I'm flat stoney-broke. Good job I spotted you following me, otherwise I wouldn't have come in here.'

'What am I getting in return?'

'One name and one address. They both belong to the meanest twelve-bar blues player I know.'

'He's in the city?'

'He's in the city.'

Montgomerie took a pound note from his hip pocket and slid it across the table but kept his finger on it.

'That'll do nicely, polis person. Try Toby McCann, 96 Atholl Gardens, G12.'

Montgomerie took his finger off the pound note and took a biro from his jacket pocket. 'You're pretty free at pointing the finger at your friends,' he said, scribbling the name and address on the newspaper.

'He's not that much of a friend,' said the man, crumpling up the note and pushing it into his own pocket. 'Besides, he's not Slow Tom. He's got black hair.'

'But he can play twelve-bar blues?'

'Polis person, he is a natural. He's trying to make it in the ents business, he's not into serious blues. He's just burning himself up looking for a break.'

'That so?' said Montgomerie.

Ninety-six Atholl Gardens was a bleak Victorian tenement. It was also damp. The dampness gripped at
Montgomerie's chest and made it feel hollow. He started
up the stairs, feeling his way one step at a time and running his hand up the bannister rail. The house was quiet,
dead quiet, and Montgomerie felt a sinister atmosphere.
He had to go to the top landing underneath a grimy
skylight before he found a door with McCann on the
front. He knocked twice on the door, gently.

There was just the loud silence of the empty stair. He
knocked again.

There was a rustling inside the flat; from the other side
of the door a voice said, 'Who's there?'

'Police,' said Montgomerie under his breath. Then
loudly he said, 'Scottish Television.' He hitched the
cassette recorder he had slung over his shoulder round to
his front. Nice of Gillian to lend it to him. But she could
hardly stop him, he was out of the door before she knew
what was happening. She had yelled after him that he
had to be bloody careful, it was a twenty-first birthday
present. He hadn't known she was as old as that.

'Who?'

'STV.'

'Minute.'

A few moments later the door opened six inches. It was
attached to the frame by a bronze chain and above the
chain a round face blinked at Montgomerie.

'STV,' said Montgomerie, smiling.

The blinking eyes moved from Montgomerie's face to
the tape recorder and back to Montgomerie's face. Montgomerie continued to smile.

'Yes?' said the man.

'I heard you were a good guitar player. I'd like to take a
sample.' He tapped the tape recorder. 'No promises, you
understand, not even of an audition, but we're anxious to
find new talent for a musical show. Should run to six

Saturday evening programmes. One established name to head the bill and new talent in support. Somebody pointed me your way.'

The door shut. Montgomerie heard the chain being unhitched. The door opened, a young man, barefoot in jeans and a vest, stood in the doorway. 'I just got up,' he said.

Montgomerie extended his hand. 'Malcolm Montgomerie. Most people call me Mal.'

'Toby McCann,' he had a thin hand with long fingers. 'Most people call me Toby.'

'Sense of humour is important,' said Montgomerie, grinning.

Toby McCann led the way down a threadbare hall carpet to a bedsitting-room. The bed was unmade, there was a Winnie the Pooh poster on the wall and a twelve-string jumbo acoustic guitar leaning against the wall.

'Where can I set the tape up, Toby?'

'Next to mine on the desk is about the best place.'

'Local talent, are you, Toby?'

'Aye, well, Dumbarton way, that's where I hail from. I'm in my first year at the university but I want to make it in the music business.'

'From what I hear you've got no problem, Toby.' Montgomerie set the machine on a table top, which was scattered with paper. On the paper was a series of scribbles, music and lyrics, the doodlings of a budding songwriter. Toby McCann took up his guitar and began to strum. Montgomerie propped the microphone against a book about Woody Guthrie.

'What do I do?' asked Toby McCann, looking bewildered.

'Oh, say something, Toby, so we can get your speaking voice, then sing one of your songs. You write your own material, don't you, Toby?'

'Oh, yes. I don't know whether it's any good, though.'

'Well, let's see,' said Montgomerie. 'You seem to have a good reputation.'

'Yeah?'

'That's right.' Montgomerie pressed the record button and stepped back from the machine.

Toby McCann strummed a few chords and then in a curiously affected voice said, 'Well, this is just a little song I wrote and I hope you like it . . . was that O.K., Mal?' Montgomerie nodded. Toby McCann sang a song about a lonely boy whom nobody understands. He finished the song and looked at Montgomerie, who was convinced he had found the hoaxer. But he was more stunned by the guitar-playing: rarely in his life had he heard more beautiful, flowing unaccompanied music or seen such fluidity of wrist movement. Toby McCann's hands seemed to have a life of their own. Half seriously Montgomerie said, 'I'd like to be your agent.'

'Can you help me, Mal?' Toby McCann looked eagerly at Montgomerie. 'Play it back, let's hear it.'

Montgomerie walked over to the machine. He looked at it and felt his stomach constrict. Flatly he said, 'There isn't a tape in the machine.'

Toby McCann leaned forward and glanced at the recorder. 'Wouldn't have made any difference, you weren't recording anyway,' he said, 'The mike jack-plug isn't home.'

'It's a new machine, Toby. Sorry.'

'It's about five years old.'

Gillian is *not* twenty-six. 'It's new to me, Toby.'

'Do you want to borrow one of my tapes?'

'I'll pay you for it.' It didn't matter if she was.

'Just let me have it back, Mal.' He tossed a tape to Montgomerie. Montgomerie put the tape in the machine and pressed the microphone plug fully into the side of the recorder. He pressed the 'record' button. Toby McCann repeated his performance and again Montgomerie stood back in awe. He had a vision of a brilliant guitarist drawing on his early experiences of arrest and imprisonment for his material. He felt he was helping to create something. Montgomerie pocketed the tape and slung the machine over his shoulder.

'I'll hear from you?' asked Toby McCann, who had just decided that 'Tobe McCann' was to be his stage name and that he was going to get a pair of tinted spectacles for when his photograph was taken for the cover of his first long-playing record.

'Aye. I'll have to play it to my governor, Mr Donoghue, but I dare say he'll like it.'

'Donoghue?' said McCann. 'I've heard that name somewhere.'

'He's a nice man,' said Montgomerie. 'A gentleman. You'll like him.'

McCann looked at him, paling a little.

Montgomerie walked back to Otago Street and dropped the machine off at Gillian's flat. She was making notes from an American textbook and offered him coffee. He declined. She didn't look twenty-six. He took a No. 16 bus into the city.

Donoghue listened to the tape, pulling gently on his pipe as he did so. Montgomerie sat in front of the table, feeling unkempt.

'I think you have him,' said Donoghue. 'We'll have to compare the voice traces, but I'd say this is our man. What's he like?'

'Short, lean, naive, but he can play a guitar like nobody I know.'

'Waste of talent, like a lot of people that keep you and me in a job.'

'I think he'll make it in the end. Get his autograph for your daughter, sir.'

The phone rang on the desk. It saved Donoghue the difficulty of telling Montgomerie that he objected to his remark. Instead he settled for a furrowed brow, picked up the phone and said, 'Hello?' Montgomerie saw Donoghue's eyebrows rise and the furrow deepen. He heard his senior say, 'Bring him up, please.'

The two men waited in silence. There was a knock on the door, Montgomerie turned round. A constable in a blue shirt stood in the doorway. Next to him stood Toby McCann. His hair was wet.

'It was only a joke,' he said.

CHAPTER 9

Richard King left Susan Smith's house at 10.30 a.m., half an hour after Sussock and Donoghue had left and one hour after the body had been taken away. He left only after Bothwell had satisfied himself that he had dusted for prints throughout the bedroom, the downstairs room where the body was found, the hall and the kitchen. Bothwell packed his equipment away, confident that he had six different sets of prints, possibly seven, in a total of one hundred and fifty-three individual traces.

'No sign of a break-in, sir,' he said, 'or I'd definitely know where to dust for the suspect prints.'

'So long as you gave the bedroom a good going over; we know he was in there,' replied King. 'How would you like a pad like this, Bothwell?'

'Cost plenty,' said the man. 'Wouldn't know where to look for my shoes.'

'Where do you stay, Bothwell?'

'Queen's Park, sir. With my mother, she's a widow. She worked as a receptionist after my dad died but she had to give that up, she fell ill, you see.'

'I'm sorry to hear that.'

'Oh, we get by,' he said, forcing a smile.

King knew that he was making Bothwell uncomfortable. 'What sort of social life do you have, Bothwell?'

'Oh, I take a pint, not had a lot of success with the girls though, sir.'

'How old are you?'

'Thirty-three.'

'Well, let us have those prints as soon as you have them mounted. Bring them straight up to the incident room, please.'

'Yes, sir,' said Bothwell and left hurriedly. King followed him, stopping briefly to speak to the constable who would be standing on duty outside the front door of the house for the next six hours until he was relieved. King stepped in Bothwell's footprints as he walked down the driveway. The sky was a cold, dull grey, a keen wind was blowing, but the snow seemed to be thawing. He found himself humming 'Good King Wenceslas' to himself. He hadn't known Bothwell was so old.

Back at P Division station King sat at his desk, pondering. He leaned back in his chair with his elbows resting on the chair arms and both index fingers pyramided against his brow. Presently he leaned forward and picked up the telephone and said, 'Computer Terminal, please . . . Computer Terminal? . . . DC King, P Division . . . sorry it's a bad line . . . K-I-N-G . . . yes . . . I'd like a breakdown of all unsolved murders of boys aged between eight and fourteen . . . F-o-u-r . . . fourteen in the west of Scotland during the last five years . . . Five, as in maids a-milking . . . well, yesterday would be nice, but could you phone me back in half an hour with a verbal? Thank you.'

He replaced the receiver and went to the basement and searched for the criminal record of one Jamie McPherson of Partick. He wrote on a red card 'McPherson, James; DC King. 25 Jan' and slipped the red card behind the file of McPherson Iain and in front of the file of McPherson John and returned to his office.

He tried to stop his pulse racing. 'Softly, softly,' he told himself and went to the canteen and made a mug of coffee before allowing himself to open the file. The previous convictions read:

AGED	PLACE OF TRIAL	COURT	OFFENCE	SENTENCE
18	Glasgow	Sheriff Summary	Breach of the Peace	fined £10
19	Glasgow	Sheriff Summary	Assault Assault to severe injury	Three months detention
20	Kilmarnock	Sheriff Summary	Con. Road Traffic Act 1960, Section 3 Con. Road Traffic Act 1960, Section 5	Fined £10
20	Glasgow	Sheriff Summary	Police Assault	Six months Y.O.I.
22	Glasgow	Sheriff Summary	Theft	28 days detention
22	Glasgow	Glasgow High Court	Attempted Murder	Three years imprisonment
25	Glasgow	Sheriff Summary	Non-payment of fine	Sixty days imprisonment
25	Paisley	Sheriff Summary	Theft	Fined £20
27	Glasgow	Sheriff Summary	Theft	Three months imprisonment

'Bad lad,' said King and sipped his coffee. In the file was a Social Background Report which had evidently been requested in connection with the Attempted Murder conviction:

Social Work Department,
West Three, Glasgow.
17th April

Report on James McPherson   age 22
of 12 Glassel Street,
Glasgow 12
Currently at H.M. Prison, Barlinnie
Offence—Attempted Murder
Court—The High Court
Date of Court 23 April
Previous Court appearances—as libelled.

FAMILY AND HOME CIRCUMSTANCES

Mr James McPherson aged 53 — Unemployed.
Father.

James McPherson aged 22 — Unemployed. Subject of this report

Sonia McPherson aged 13 — Scholar. Sister.

The family live in a three-room flat in the West End of the city. It is untidy but not especially unclean and tends to reflect a warm and 'lived-in' environment. Mr McPherson (senior) has not worked for some years since he sustained a severe back injury at his place of work. Although he can walk he is only able to take a limited number of steps at a time and so is virtually housebound. He also has a severe chest complaint which further hinders his mobility. Mr McPherson blames himself for his son's criminal activities in that he sees his injury and resulting incapacitation as having prevented him from being a father to his son. He has similar worries about Sonia's future. Mr McPherson's wife, who was apparently a very powerful figure in the family, died when James McPherson (subject) was eleven.

The income of the McPherson household is derived entirely from statutory sources.

PERSONAL HISTORY

James McPherson (subject) was born in Greenock and moved to Glasgow with his family when he was seven. He attended local primary and secondary modern schools (where he received remedial education) and left at 15 years with no qualifications. He reports great distress at the death of his mother and says that this incident started his drinking which in turn led to his criminal career. The writer understands that his previous offences were all alcohol-related.

Mr McPherson (subject) has a patchy work record. He worked as a van-boy with a bakery for three months before leaving it in favour of a job as a porter in the meat market. He was dismissed from this post but refused to give details about the circumstances surrounding his dismissal. His last job was that of a labourer, which he lost following his committal to the Young Offenders Institution eighteen months ago.

THE OFFENCE

The offence took place after a drinking session on a Saturday night. The company, of which Mr McPherson (subject) was a member, left the bar and went to a flat, which belonged to one of the group, in order to consume the carry-outs they had purchased. During the course of the evening one member of the group accused Mr McPherson (subject) of having homosexual leanings. Mr McPherson then produced a flick-knife and attempted to stab the person who made the remark. He had to be restrained until the police arrived.

James McPherson (subject) related the incident in a quiet, matter-of-fact manner, and admitted that he would have killed unless prevented. Regrettably the writer was unable to detect any evidence of contrition on the part of Mr McPherson (subject).

Peter Stringer
Social Worker.

'Got a temper, too,' said King and drained the coffee from his mug. He leaned forward and picked up the phone and asked for the computer terminal. He identified himself and asked, 'Anything for me yet?' What they had for him were eight unsolved murders of young boys in the west of Scotland over the last five years. King matched the time of each murder against McPherson's criminal record and found that he had been at liberty when five of the murders were committed. Of those five murders one boy was battered to death and a second had been poisoned (this death was query misadventure). These two varied in age by a factor of four years, one being ten and the other being fourteen. There was an interval of five years separating the two murders and a distance of two hundred miles separating the location of each murder. They were undoubtedly murdered by different persons.

The three remaining murders interested King greatly. They were murders of boys who were of the same age; two were eleven and one was three months short of eleven. All three had been raped before or shortly after being strangled. The murders had taken place in the Glasgow area over a period of five years and King felt embarrassed for his profession that the pattern had not been noticed before. The press hadn't noticed either, but that, King felt, was cold comfort. There was a definite pattern: age, sex, method and location all pointed to the three boys being murdered by the same person. King checked the dates of the three murders against Jamie McPherson's file. The boys had each been murdered within six weeks of Jamie McPherson being released from custody.

King closed the file and drummed his fingers on it. So far there was no evidence, not even circumstantial, that McPherson was the murderer. He saw no reason to bring McPherson in, no need to alarm him into flight, no point in allowing him time to fix an alibi. King knew that if he rushed this he'd have to wrestle it all the way to the Procurator Fiscal's office. There didn't seem to be a matter of urgency, either; if McPherson was true to his established pattern he wouldn't murder again until he was next released from prison. King reopened the file and recorded his suspicions and reasons for not moving directly against Jamie McPherson. He wrote a memo to Donoghue detailing the similarities of the three murders and his suspicion that they were all the victims of one man. He dropped it in the NON-URGENT typing basket. In the file on the McAlpine boy he wrote 'Cross refer—James McPherson—GPM 13271' for the collator. He returned Jamie McPherson's file to the basement, scored his name off the red card after replacing the file, and went to the incident room.

There was a constable in the room manning the telephone, and he stood as King entered the room. King waved him down. On the table was a cellophane envelope containing six sets of fingerprints, marked A to F. Clipped to the outside of the envelope was an official compliment slip on which a round hand had written, A—Deceased; B—Cleaning lady; C,D,E,F—checked with National Police Computer—No trace; E—Bothwell.

'No trace,' said King. 'That's all we need.'

It was just midday. He pulled on his coat and went out for lunch.

At 2.15 that afternoon, Fabian Donoghue sat in front of a row of reporters and two television cameras. He wondered if this was going to be the one he was going to blow, the one he was going to learn from, and he felt his stomach tighten. He had chased men over rooftops in the moonlight, he had been held prisoner for hours with a shotgun held against his chest, he had jumped into a freezing river at dead of night to rescue a drowning child who on closer inspection revealed himself to be a half-submerged inner-tube, but the only situation which frightened him was that period just before a press conference. It wasn't so bad when he was in there and pitchin', it was those awful moments before the starting whistle. The constable on the door was looking at him, the reporters had stopped shuffling and were waiting, fingers poised over their cassette recorders. The camera crew had set the definition and the lens apertures. Twenty-five people waited for him to start the conference. He thought that it wouldn't be so bad if he didn't have to blow the damn whistle himself. Finally he raised his head and said, 'Thank you, Constable.'

The camera crew bent forward, the reporters pressed buttons on their recorders and reached for their notebooks.

'Gentlemen,' he began, 'thank you for coming. As you know, this conference concerns the killer known as Slow Tom and I have called this particular conference to keep you abreast of the situation. I'm afraid the news is not good. I'll take questions, but not until I have finished speaking, please.'

He paused. But not long enough to overdo it.

'The number of murders committed by the killer has now risen to five and we are no nearer to making an arrest than we were two weeks ago. We know nothing more about this man than we did a few hours after the murder of Patrick Duffy.

'Last week a tape recording and photocopies of a letter were released to the press. These both came from a man who called himself Slow Tom and who claimed to be the killer. This enabled us to narrow the field of suspects considerably but subsequently this man proved to be a hoaxer.'

The reporters groaned and talked among themselves. A few arms were raised but Donoghue held out his hand, palm outward. The arms retracted.

'A man has been arrested and will appear before the Glasgow Sheriff tomorrow morning charged with wasting police time. The situation then is that we are at Square One again; we don't know what the murderer looks or sounds like, we don't even have the dubious comfort of a promise to stop at nine victims.

'The killer's *modus operandi* has changed, probably in a response to our early warnings about not staying out late or going out alone, preferably not doing either. The killer has taken to pursuing his victims to their homes. The last two victims were ladies, both murdered in their homes, and in one case, that of a young woman whose body was found just this morning, we believe that the killer was ac-

tually waiting for her inside her house when she returned
home late last night.'

In front of him Donoghue saw heads sag forward. One
reporter clutched his stomach.

'I'm afraid I can't say anything else about his latest
victim, I haven't yet heard whether the relatives have
been informed. We believe that this particular lady kept
her key under her front door mat; there's an obvious
lesson there, so I won't labour the point, nevertheless I
can't urge ladies strongly enough to have their boy-friends
look around their flat before they say good night. If he
stays the night so much the better. Most of his victims
seem to be women and so a certain pattern is being built
up, but the sadness of it is that women are not now safe in
their homes. If a woman hasn't got anyone to go out with
who will return with her, I urge her then to stay in. All
adult women seem to be potential targets, the youngest
victim was in her early twenties and the oldest in her
sixties.'

He paused. He felt he needed the pause. He hadn't
anything else to say anyway. The reporters didn't look
eager; most had wide eyes and hanging jaws.

'I'll take questions, one at a time, please.'

A reporter raised his hand.

'Does this mean you'll be calling in Scotland Yard,
Inspector?'

'No.'

A bearded man with a distended stomach asked, 'Does
the Inspector agree with the view that the killer is an
escapee from an institution for the criminally insane?'

'No he doesn't,' replied Donoghue, shortly. It was a
stupid question and he was irritated by its formality.
'Neither Carstairs nor Broadmoor have reported such a
patient escaping within recent years. Next.'

'In fact, what you're really saying, Inspector, is that
despite five murders you know nothing about the killer

save his hair colour and his type of overcoat and his blood group?'

'In fact, yes,' said Donoghue. 'Next.'

'What will your next move be, Inspector?'

If Donoghue knew that he'd crack the case. 'We know little about this man,' he said. 'We are following any leads that we come across, even if they take us to a hoaxer. But the reality is that we have to wait for this man to make a slip, to leave a fingerprint, to be seen, that's the thing we really need, a sighting, we haven't had anybody come forward, despite five murders, who can say that they saw something and so we can't make up a photofit. All we can do at the moment is to play a defensive game. Make it hard for him. Don't go out alone, especially if you are a woman—but men are not immune either—scream and run if you are attacked, have someone come home with you to check your house. Don't go out at all if possible.'

'Is your journey really necessary?' It was said by one of the reporters; he intended it to be a joke in a stressful situation, but no-one laughed.

'That's about it,' said Donoghue, grimly.

In fact the killer had been seen. Benjamin Strachan was a retired architect and he lived two houses down from Susan Smith's and on the opposite side of the road. A plumbline-stretch of one hundred yards from his front gate to hers. Benjamin Strachan was a man of habit and went to bed at 10.30 each night, no matter what film was on television, no matter what social function might require his attendance. His head would be on the pillow at 10.31 and his eyes would be shut at 10.45. He was a lifelong teetotaller and a lay preacher.

He had 20:20 vision.

At 10.15 he was standing at his bedroom window. The window was frosting over and outside the snow was driving down thickly. He glimpsed a black shape making its way diagonally across the front lawn of Susan Smith's house.

He thought it was a large dog.

The press conference made the later editions of the evening press and the 6 p.m. news on the radio and the television stations. Donoghue felt he needed to get out of the station, he just wanted out, he needed a brief respite before he could go on with banging his head relentlessly against a brick wall. He decided to walk up Sauchiehall Street and back. He winced as he passed the paper-sellers' stands and the newsagents' shops:

POLICE SAY SLOW TOM IS A HOAX

POLICE SAY THE GAME IS DEFENSIVE

POLICE KNOW NOTHING

TAKE YOUR MAN HOME, SAY POLICE

One man had a pitch at the corner of Renfield and Sauchiehall. He was standing in a plastic mackintosh, the snow melted on it, he had a hat and his papers were covered with a polythene sheet. He was standing in three inches of slush. Donoghue bought a paper from him so that the other people in the street wouldn't think that he was a policeman. He went back down Sauchiehall Street and stopped in at the 51st State Diner. He took a single table and ordered an American beer and what his daughter would call a 'double pigburger'.

He missed his family.

Donoghue read the paper while he waited for the girl in the red T-shirt and denim shorts to bring his meal to him. The pages were soggy and he had to peel them apart. On the inside page was an open letter from Bill Cowan, crime reporter:

I'll call you Jim. I don't know what your real name is, but you know who I'm talking to, don't you, Jim? Listen, Jim, I'm on your side. I'm sitting up and I'm listening. I want you to tell me what you want to say because I think you've got something to say but you aren't doing it right.

See, Jim, you've knifed four women—three of them were very young—and one man. What have you proved? What have you said? Tell me, Jim. Jim, you're ill. You need help. We know you exist, Jim, you've scared this city like nothing ever known, you've shaken us to our roots, have you been on the streets and seen the way strangers look at each other? All because of you, Jim.

Jim, I want you to find a police station and walk into it. I want you to give yourself up so we can give you the help you need, and you need it desperately, Jim.

This is for you and me, Jim.   B.C.

Donoghue thought it might even work; it certainly deserved to work. The waitress smiled and slipped Donoghue's meal in front of him. Donoghue needed that smile.

Benjamin Strachan slept well the night he saw what he took to be a large dog crossing Susan Smith's lawn. The next day his suspicions were aroused when he saw men walking in and out of her house, an ambulance waiting at the kerb, the cleaning lady being helped into a car and at the end of it a solitary policeman in a cape standing at her door. Benjamin Strachan took an afternoon nap and missed the earliest bulletins at midday.

The first he knew of the incident was when he watched the early evening broadcasts on the television which named the name and showed a picture of the house. He stood up, crossed his living-room, went into the hall and picked up the telephone. He dialled the number which had been flashed on his television screen.

'I'd like to talk to someone about the murder,' he said. 'I have a bad chest and I can't leave the house this

weather. Can someone visit me?' He gave his address.
    Malcolm Montgomerie was there in fifteen minutes.

Benjamin Strachan's house was dark and calm and quiet
and ordered. It made Montgomerie walk softly and talk
quietly. Benjamin Strachan took Montgomerie's coat and
hung it on the hall bannister. He led the way into the
front room and indicated a deep and heavy armchair
near to the hearth in which burned a small coal fire. The
curtains were half-closed, the furniture was old and dark
and the table was draped with a green velvet cloth. The
room smelled of the solid smell which Montgomerie had
come to associate with age and well-earned rest. The light
came from a lamp which glowed dimly by the doorway.
    Benjamin Strachan left the room and Montgomerie
heard the clatter of tea cups and saucers and a kettle
whistling. It was obvious that Benjamin Strachan was
going to dictate the pace of the interview and so Montgomerie relaxed and settled into the armchair. He noticed
that the hearth was composed of pictorial tiles. When the
man returned to the room he was carrying a wicker tray
on which were two cups, sugar in a bowl and milk in a
matching jug, and a small teapot covered with a knitted
cosy. He asked Montgomerie if he took milk and sugar.
'Just milk,' said Montgomerie. He took the cup and
saucer, raising himself slightly from his chair, and as he
did so noticed that the old man's movements were as deft
and steady as any twenty-year-old's. He was a tall, thin
man with short grey hair and a lean face which seemed
ingrained with wisdom and understanding. He wore a
shaggy green pullover and Montgomerie imagined his
arms to be strong and sinewy. Benjamin Strachan sat
down effortlessly in the other armchair and Montgomerie
wondered if the man had been an athlete in his youth.
    'I don't get a lot of visitors, young man,' said Benjamin
Strachan. He had a smooth, easy-on-the-ear voice. 'So we

are really helping each other.' He smiled.

'How long have you been on your own, sir?'

'My wife died six years ago. Our son lives in Canada. He's a senior partner in a Toronto-based firm of architects.'

'Really,' said Montgomerie and sipped his tea.

'I have a few friends, in the church mostly, and some good neighbours. They send their children round to see me and to run errands for me. Things like that are touching to a man of my years. I'm eighty-three.'

'Christ,' hissed Montgomerie.

'I'm a lifelong teetotaller and non-smoker. Mind you, I did take a cigarette at the Armistice Party in 1918. I didn't like it. I was very young at the time, still at school, I believe.'

'It certainly seems to have paid off,' said Montgomerie. 'I feel bound to say that you look remarkably fit.'

'It isn't something to boast about, young man, more something to be thankful for, and I'm not sure it has paid off; my generation is dead, and I think you have to live and die with your own generation. I don't feel I belong any more. I've overstayed my welcome. I believe I know where we go when we die and I believe my friends and my dear wife are waiting for me. I shall see them some day.' The man stirred his tea, even though he hadn't sweetened it. 'But if you want longevity in your life, I advise no smoking or drinking and a good nourishing sleep. A healthy routine is the thing. I was at my routine when I saw the strange sight last night.'

'Would you like to tell me about it, sir?' Montgomerie put his cup on the floor and took out his notebook.

'I was looking out of my bedroom window as I always do before I do my exercises. My bedroom is the room above this one and looks out on to the road. The time was two or three minutes either side of ten-fifteen.'

Montgomerie scribbled on his pad.

'It was snowing thickly and my windows were rimmed with frost, nevertheless I could see Miss Smith's house very clearly and I noticed a black shape crossing her lawn.'

'A shape?'

'I took it to be a dog, it might still have been a dog, you understand, I am saying that I saw something which may or may not have been connected with the sad incident which took place last night, and which I only learned about an hour ago.'

'I understand.'

'It was a black shape and it went diagonally across the lawn. It climbed from the road, on to the wall and went across the lawn towards the front door.'

'What happened when it reached the front door, sir?'

'I didn't see it reach the door. I only saw it going in the direction of the front door. It didn't use the drive and so I thought it was a stray. I had a mind to go and bring it in for the night but I thought that it would be long gone by the time I reached Miss Smith's house and so I turned from the window to attend to my exercises.'

'Can you describe it, please?'

'Well I said I thought it was a dog because that's the only thing I thought it could be. The visibility was poor and I only had a fleeting glimpse, but if I am to be completely honest the gait of what I saw put me in mind of a monkey.'

'A monkey?'

'An ape, then. It sort of rolled across the lawn, I'm using the word figuratively, it had a rapid, rolling gait. I thought I could not have seen an ape and so I decided that I had seen a large dog.'

'Large?'

'About the height of a Great Dane. I had a Great Dane once. Magnificent beast.'

Delicately Montgomerie enquired about Benjamin Strachan's vision.

'I have perfect vision, young man. I'm also fairly observant. Did you know that one of the decorative cuff-buttons on your overcoat is missing?'

Montgomerie confessed he didn't know.

Montgomerie thanked the old man and drove back to P Division. He tracked Donoghue down in the canteen and told him about Benjamin Strachan and what Benjamin Strachan had said.

'What do you think?' said Donoghue, sipping his coffee.

'He seems *compos mentis*, sir, and he could see better than I could in that room.'

'He probably knew where everything was, like a blind person would. If you moved his chair six inches to one side he'd sit on the arm.'

'Probably, sir. But I didn't get that impression.'

'I don't think it gives us any leads. Was he an old man asking for attention?'

'He was old, but not desperately lonely. I think he was sincere. He seemed to take himself very seriously, he wasn't the sort that could make wild claims so that he could entertain somebody.'

'Write it up and file it. Chimps with kitchen knives, that takes the cake.'

'Perhaps it's been specially trained,' suggested Montgomerie with a grin.

Donoghue rose and rinsed his cup. 'I wish you'd stop making jokes, Montgomerie,' he said with a frown. He had left his car at home and was using the train because that day he had a terror of an ice-bound M8. It was 7.30. If he got the eight o'clock he'd be home by 9.30. 'You'll be on your own tonight,' he said to Montgomerie. 'Ray Sussock's phoned in sick, he's gone down with a cold. He may be in tomorrow, but right now I imagine he's snug and warm with a strong toddy inside him. If you need support King is on call. The desk sergeant has the list of uniforms and if he strikes, be he man or be he ape, pick up the phone and call me immediately. I'll get in somehow.'

'Yes, sir,' said Montgomerie, awed at the responsibility that had just been thrust upon him.

Tomorrow night I have an appointment with the Welfare Lady. Lissu said I could. I made the appointment for five o'clock, for after my work, as if I go to my work . . . ha, ha, ha, ha . . . She said did I need to come? Couldn't I discuss it over the telephone? I said I needed to see her. After work, I said. She gave me an appointment for five o'clock. She's old and has a stiff hairdo and she thinks she does me favours. Tomorrow I'm going to take my friend with me.

CHAPTER 10

The solitary figure solidified out of the shadows and walked slowly down the street. The street was dark, there was slush underfoot, the buildings at either side of the street were derelict. The man thought this city was a bitch. A wild, red-haired Irish bitch. She had the long flowing hair of the Campsies, two long limbs which lay either side of the river and met at the intimacy of the grid system at her centre. This city would love you or hate you, but she would never be indifferent to you. Not this bitch. The solitary figure was a policeman. His name was Hamilton and he knew he'd never leave her, not this bitch.

It was 2.30 in the morning of January the 26th. The temperature was nudging two degrees above freezing. Hamilton's feet slid through the ankle-deep slush, it looked like a thaw had set in, he hoped it was *the* thaw. But it wasn't warm enough to prevent his ears pinching and to prevent his breath hanging in the air like saloon-bar smoke.

Hamilton didn't care, he wouldn't have been too concerned if summer had been cancelled and the next Ice Age was making its way down Renfield Street. Tonight he felt sixteen feet tall, away tae hell, he felt twenty feet tall, tonight his chest was big, but big, tonight the slush was air and he was walking on it. Tonight his wife had told him she was pregnant. He thought this bitch of a city was a good one to bring a child up in.

He wanted a son. He'd call him Davey, after his own dad.

Hamilton saw a figure in the road ahead of him. Two hundred yards away. The figure staggered. Hamilton's pulse began to race and his stomach tightened. He quickened his pace and felt in his trouser pocket for his truncheon. The figure became a man, a short man in a raincoat too big for him. The man moved towards Hamilton, beckoning him as he did so.

'In the midden, sir,' said the man when he was within earshot. His jaw glistened with days' growth of whiskers and his breath was hot from ten feet. 'In the midden,' he said again. He grabbed Hamilton's arm. Hamilton shrugged him off.

'What's in the midden?' he asked, releasing his grip on his truncheon.

'My bed, under my doss.' The man gasped for breath and coughed deeply. The thin air was torturing his lungs. 'This way.'

Hamilton walked after the man, keeping pace with him, and he heard layers of paper creasing under the man's coat as he ran with tiny hobbling steps. The man's boots were tied with string. He stopped at the entrance of a derelict tenement; the corrugated iron sheet over the doorway had been kicked down.

'In there, sir. Dead body.'

Hamilton stepped forward and shone his torch into the close mouth. The steps were worn down, the paint was peeling, the tiles were chipped and the sandstone was pitted. Through the close he could see the dereliction of the waste ground which had once been back courts. The air stank of urine, even at 2° Centigrade.

'Top flat,' said the man.

'Top!'

'Aye.'

'The stairs O.K., aye?'

'Aye.'

Hamilton turned his head and spoke into his radio. 'Poppa Control, this is P246, Constable Hamilton.'

'Control receiving.' The radio crackled. On the river a ship was moving. Its foghorn blast rolled heavily over the rooftops.

'Control. Am entering derelict property at . . .' he peered at the flaking paint on the stonework outside the close mouth but couldn't discern the numbers . . . 'At two-thirds of the way along Caledonia Street proceeding south from Glasgow Cross. Am investigating report of dead body. Assistance required. Over.'

'Control. Wait until assistance arrives. Over.'

'Understood,' said Hamilton and flicked off his radio.

'What's your name then, Jim?' he asked, taking out his notebook.

'Alexander McCaig, sir.'

'Where do you live?'

'Top flat, sir.'

'So this body wasn't there last night?'

'Couldn't say, sir. I've been on furlough for a week.'

'On where?'

'Furlough.'

'You mean you haven't been there for a week?'

'Aye, sir.'

'And you discovered this body when you returned the night, aye?'

'Aye.'

'What sort of body is it?'

'Dead, sir. It's a dead body.'

'I mean, is it a man or woman?'

'No, sir?'

'What?'

'It's not a man or a woman.'

'What is it then, a tailor's dummy?'

'No, sir. It's a wee boy.'

A car slowly turned the corner. It was white with a yellow flash and had a blue revolving light on the roof. It could only have come from the next street. Hamilton flashed his torch and the car drove alongside Hamilton and Alexander McCaig. It halted smoothly and quietly. Two constables in flat white caps got out.

'Report of a dead body on the top landing,' said Hamilton.

'Stairs safe?' asked one of the constables.

'Apparently,' Hamilton answered. 'But we'd better be careful.'

'Would you like to sit in the car, Jim?' said the other constable and held the rear door open. McCaig slid on to the back seat, seeming pleased to be part of the team.

'What do we do now?' asked Hamilton.

'We go and investigate. One stays with the car and him, the other two go up and check it out. Two will have to go up because we may need to corroborate the evidence about the discovery,' said the driver of the car, a constable called Piper who was junior to Hamilton, and who Hamilton thought was well on his way to becoming a sergeant.

'Yes,' said Hamilton, and very nearly added, 'sir'.

Hamilton and Piper started up the stair. In the car the other constable took out his notebook.

'Mr McCaig, is it?'

'Aye, sir. Sandy McCaig.'

'Sandy, is it? How old are you, Sandy?'

'Twenty-three, sir.'

The constable turned round and gave Sandy McCaig a cold stare. Sandy McCaig beamed at him.

'What do you do for a living, Sandy?'

'I'm in the army, sir.'

'Oh?'

'I'm a dispatch-rider with Field Marshal Montgomery. I'm on furlough at the moment. Off to the desert soon.'

The constable shut his notebook and took out a packet of cigarettes. 'Smoke, Sandy?'

'I don't mind if I do,' said Sandy McCaig.

The stairs were dark and damp. They were so dark that Hamilton's torch had little spill and he could only see clearly what the main part of the beam lit. Everything else was blackness. The windows on the stairway had been sheeted over with corrugated iron and the doors of the flats had been bricked up. It didn't prevent the rats from getting in, their scratching, bouncing, rhythmic footfall echoed in the empty rooms. Hamilton shivered. He felt he could reach out and grab the dampness, the sour smell filled his nostrils and made his chest feel hollow. He pressed on. His son would need someone to look up to.

The stairway was four floors high. At the topmost landing the bricks at the entrance of one flat had been knocked in at the centre, resembling a doorway in a ship.

Hamilton and Piper stepped over the lip of the doorway and into the flat. They shone their torches down the hallway. It was a large flat; five, probably six rooms; the plaster had fallen off the walls, the doors hung loose on hinges, there were holes in the floorboards, and where there were no holes the boards sagged under their weight.

'Careful how you go,' said Hamilton.

'I always am,' answered Piper drily.

Hamilton let that go and began to walk down the hall, testing the floor with his front foot before shifting all his weight from his back foot. On the wall was a portrait; Hamilton's torch beam picked it out, a sepia print of a young woman who was looking downcast and holding a bunch of flowers. She was in an oval frame.

In the room at the end of the hall, the room which may have been the parents' bedroom or the living-room, they found some empty cartons of cereal, some empty milk-bottles, a plastic dish and a metal spoon, a pile of dusty and empty wine-bottles, and a mound of sacking.

The head of a boy was sticking out from under the sacking. The eyes were open. That made it worse, the eyes glistening like that in the torch-beams.

Hamilton and Piper pulled back the sacking. The body was naked. Hamilton turned his torch away, but Piper continued to shine his on the boy, playing the beam along the length of the body, the folded-up legs and the bloodied anus.

'Hope I never find out who did this,' said Piper in a voice as chilly as the night. 'I've got a little brother about his age.'

Hamilton said, 'Just put the sacking back, for God's sake.'

They shone their torches about the room. Scattered on the floor were the boy's clothing; shoes, thick socks, pullover, shirt, a parka with a furry hood. In the pocket of the jeans they found a Transcard and a membership card of a youth club. The photograph on the Transcard was that of the boy who now lay underneath a pile of damp hemp, with his eyes open. The same name was on both cards: Ronald McAlpine.

The duty sergeant was a Sergeant Anderson and he checked the missing persons register. Ronald McAlpine's name had been entered on the register when his file was

opened five days ago and it stood as an example of the
grim statistic that if a missing person isn't found within 48
hours of being reported missing, the chances of their
being found alive are a slim one in ten. Phil Hamilton
stood in front of Sergeant Anderson and wrote the address of the McAlpine family in his notebook. He looked
up, white-faced. 'Off you go, lad,' said Anderson. It was
3.20 a.m.

At 7.30 Montgomerie called King at home.

'Would have called you earlier, mate,' said Montgomerie. 'But it didn't seem an emergency. We found the
body of the McAlpine boy in the night. The case was
cross-indexed to Jamie McPherson and out to you. I read
the file, looks like you've netted a big one, you'll have
your stripes up this afternoon all right. Anyway, I saw the
pace you're moving at so I didn't think it would be
necessary to get you out of bed at three in the morning.'

'Thanks, Mal. I appreciate that.' King was standing at
the unpainted doorway of his kitchen. His children were
midway through the process of transferring porridge from
their bowls to the table top. His wife was at the sink, in
her housecoat. King thought her hair was a mess. Tinny
music came out of a red transistor radio.

'The boys at the Path. Lab. and Forensics are going
over the place where he was found.'

'Where was that?'

'Some old guy's doss down near the Barrows. What
time will you be in? You're not on duty until two this
afternoon.'

'What time do you expect the reports?'

'Forensic should be any time now, mate. Dr Reynolds
has his typed up by a dolly secretary who doesn't start
work until nine so he should send his over by ten at the
latest. Mind you, he'll give a verbal to Hamilton, who's at
the Path. Lab. now.'

'Do the parents know?'

'Yes, Hamilton told them.'

'Hamilton again?'

'Uh-huh. He went from the parents' house straight to the Path. Lab.'

'He's not having an easy time, that lad.'

'He's not. In fact, wasn't it him who found the first two bodies left by our other friend?'

'That's right; I hope he's in for the kill, if and when it comes; he deserves it. Quiet night otherwise, was it?'

'Like a grave.'

'That's not funny, Mal. Anyway, thanks, I'll be in at nine.'

He was in at 8.30. He hung his hat and coat on the peg, pulled his sodden trousers from his knees and went to the canteen and made himself a coffee. In his pigeonhole were two circulars, one about saving fuel, the other about annual health checks, and reports from Hamilton, Piper and the Forensic Department. He let the circulars lie and took the reports to his desk.

Phil Hamilton's report was a what, why, when, how, where and who, blow-by-blow account of the discovery of the body. It was completely corroborated by Piper's report, but Piper's report had more depth and more comment. Piper, who knew nothing of the finger of suspicion pointing unwaveringly at Jamie McPherson, had thought fit to help the C.I.D. in every way possible and he reported that the boy *seemed* to be dead, but no cause of death was immediately obvious. However, he reported, death may have been caused by strangulation, because there was bruising around the throat, or it may have been shock because the boy *appeared* to have been raped. It was very cold in the building, read the report, but death by hypothermia could be ruled out because, although the body was naked, (a) it had been lying under a mound of sacking, (b) he had not been restrained in any way and his clothes were easily within his reach. Piper also noted that the clothes were scattered and torn but were not blood-stained and therefore suggested that the clothes had been completely removed before the boy was raped.

King put the report down, impressed.

The third report had come from the Forensic Department:

> Strathclyde Police,
> Forensic Science Unit.
> Jan 26

R. King
P Division
for information: C.P., R.D., G.F.

Report on body discovered at 27 Caledonian Road
on 26 Jan

(1) Location of body: top flat in derelict tenement property. Used for rough sleeping by vagrants.
(2) Samples taken of dust from floor and fibres from sacking for later comparison if required.
(3) Three different sets of fingerprints found. Please see attached transparencies. NPC read-out on prints to be forwarded.

It was signed, neatly, J. Bothwell.

Clipped to the report was a manilla envelope in which were six black-and-white photographs of the body and the room and the sacking and the clothes strewn across the floorboards. The photographs were still tacky. Also in the envelope were transparencies of three different fingerprints, marked A, B and C. A typewritten note explained:

Print A: Found on bottles, paper packages, dish, spoon, door of room. Multiple traces.
Print B: Found on doorway, left shoe. Two traces.
Print C: Found on shoes, Transcard and youth club pass. Multiple traces.

King didn't think he need wait for the NPC data on the

prints. He went to the basement and signed the file on Jamie McPherson out to himself and returned with it to his office. He checked the information in the file. Print B was Jamie McPherson's left thumbprint.

King went to the canteen and made himself another mug of coffee. He was shaking slightly, and wanted to calm himself. He carried the coffee back towards his office, glancing in at the front office as he passed, where the Wagnerian form of Elka Willems was slipping a sheet of paper into his pigeonhole. He went into the office and retrieved the paper: it was a report from Dr Reynolds of the Glasgow Royal Infirmary. Back at his desk King sipped the coffee and read the report.

Glasgow Royal Infirmary
Department of Clinical Pathology.
26 January

The Chief Superintendent,
Strathclyde Police
P Division
G.3

Preliminary report on an examination of body
believed to be that of Ronald McAlpine,
aged ten years and nine months.

(1) Body that of young male of European extraction. Apparent age eleven years.

(2) Rigor mortis established. Clinical signs of early decomposition noticed on extremities.

(3) Isolated pinpoint contusions to neck. Indicate strangulation.

(4) Sock found lodged in trachea.

(5) Tearing of anal tissue. Excessive haemorrhaging in anal area.

(6) Contusions to buttocks, lower lumbar region, left shoulder blade.

(7) Abrasions to chest, knees and forehead.

(8) Time of death approximately four days prior to
    body being examined. Cold weather arrested
    rate of decomposition.
    Was subject to non-accidental death. Was sexually
assaulted. Death caused by strangulation and asphyxi-
ation. Blood in anal region indicates assault before death
or up to thirty minutes after.

D. Reynolds
Pathologist

Richard King drove out to Partick. The roads were deep
in slush, snow fell lazily but relentlessly in the still air.
Behind him was a transit van in which were two policemen of mountainous proportions. King didn't think he'd
need them, but was comforted by their presence.

He pulled up outside the close in which the McPhersons
lived and glanced up the street to the McAlpine
household. Their curtains were shut, as were their
neighbours' curtains, a mark of respect for the bereaved
and the departed. He was pleased they were shut, it
reduced the chances of the McAlpines witnessing the
arrest. Glassel Road would know about Jamie McPherson
soon enough; King just wanted a quick and un-
complicated arrest.

He went to the door alone and knocked on it, twice. It
was opened by Sonia McPherson, sallow and white, who
eyed him suspiciously. From the living-room came the
sound of a cartoon show on television. So early in the
morning for television.

'Is your brother in, Sonia?' asked King.

'Aye.'

The television was turned down.

'Who is it?' A rough male voice yelled from the living-
room, and then began coughing.

'Man for Jamie.' Sonia turned and shouted down the
corridor, but kept her hand on the door.

'C'min.' The man yelled in the midst of coughing.

Sonia let her hand slip from the door and stepped aside. King walked down the corridor and into the living-room. The fire was banked high, the old man sat in a high chair and heaved into a handkerchief. In the corner of the room a muted Bugs Bunny ran into a rock face. Jamie McPherson lay on a sleeping-bag, he was smoking a cigarette and on the floor at his side was a half-drunk cup of tea. He looked at King, curious, frightened. In the sleeping bag he looked like a girl.

King felt something rise in him. He checked it. He told himself that this was going to be smooth and non-violent, his ideal; like the arrest of the boys who were stripping lead from the roof of Royston Baptist Chapel.

'Hi, Jamie,' he said.

'Mr King.'

'We found the boy, Jamie, young Ronnie McAlpine, and we know about the others.'

The room was silent. Sonia and the old man looked at Jamie McPherson with wide eyes.

'I didn't want to kill him, Mr King, not any of them. But they wouldn't keep quiet. I kept asking him for days, just to come for a walk with me, but he wouldn't. I waited for him outside the club and took him with me. I had the lend of a van. After prison, I mean, I had to do it to someone else . . .'

'Get your clothes on, Jamie,' said King.

The girl started to cry. The man tried to say something, but he could only cough. Bugs Bunny chewed a carrot and the television screen said, 'That's all, folks.' Donoghue's day started in the Glasgow Sheriff Court at 149 Ingram Street. He had always felt the building to be grim and claustrophobic and he was always anxious to reduce his time there to a minimum. That morning he was giving evidence in the trial of Toby McCann. The hearing was pleasingly short; McCann had entered a guilty plea which was accepted and he was remanded for three weeks for reports. He was taken to the cells to await transport to Longriggend. Donoghue rose, bowed to the Sheriff, and left the building to walk across the city to P Division. He knew that young McCann would spend the next three weeks dressed in blue overalls being marched everywhere. He would mature rapidly.

That day Donoghue received two telephone calls. Both upset him and one annoyed him. The first call was taken shortly after 11 a.m.

'Gentleman by the name of Payne on the line, sir,' said the constable on the switchboard. 'Wants to speak to you.'

'Put him on, please,' said Donoghue, and after the clicking of the line said, 'Sam, hello, what can I do for you?'

'Hello, Inspector. I think I've found Lissu for you.'

Donoghue's heart stopped. He picked up his pen.

'Where?' he asked.

'Devon.'

'Devon?'

'It's a beautiful county.'

'I know. Where in Devon?'

'Exeter.'

'Do you have an address?'

'No.'

'How did you find him?' Donoghue was by now more curious about the lack of urgency in Sam Payne's voice than he was excited at the prospect of receiving invaluable information.

'Through a friend of mine, Inspector. I told him about Lissu and he said it sounded Oriental. He asked a friend of his who's at Exeter University. This guy at Exeter is a Chemistry teacher by trade, but he just happens to be an expert in Chinese history. Ancient Chinese history, that is.'

Donoghue thought he detected a faint grudge in Sam Payne's voice. He hoped he was wrong.

'Anyway, this guy phoned up this morning and tells us

that Lissu is probably spelled L-i, one word, capital S-s-u, second word. Li-Ssu, you see, two words.'

'Go on,' said Donoghue scribbling.

'Li-Ssu was the chief Minister of the Emperor Chi'in and he trod the boards around 230 BC. Anyway, Li-Ssu spent a lot of time destroying the cultures of other dynasties. He was a bit of a Göebbels in his day.'

'Trust you to come up with a Nazi, Sam.'

'Speaking of which, would you help us out, Inspector?'

'If I can.'

'We have meetings, we plan, we try to keep it secret, but the law's always one step ahead of us. Do you operate phone taps on political organizations, Inspector?'

'Sam, I don't know, and I couldn't tell you if I did know what the South Yorkshire Police do.'

'Don't expect you could, Mr Donoghue. Well, I'll see you around.'

The tone in Sam Payne's voice was stronger and Donoghue knew that Sam Payne was telling him something. He was telling him that their collaboration was over, that once again they were on opposite sides of the fence. Donoghue wanted to say, 'Wait, Sam. I don't think that way, all police are not like that,' but it all seemed so useless. It seemed that Sam Payne wanted him in that role and Donoghue could do nothing about it.

'So long, Sam,' he said, and put the receiver down. He felt a sense of something lost.

He recorded the content of the telephone conversation in the file and from the file he removed a photograph of the mirror in Susan Smith's bedroom. The photograph was in close-up and clearly showed the words 'This is for Lissu.' He slipped the photograph into an envelope, lit his pipe and left the office, to keep an appointment he had made with Mr Simpson of the Applied Psychology Department of Glasgow University. He was heavy-hearted; the telephone conversation with Sam Payne had upset him.

'I should have done this earlier, sir,' said Donoghue.
'Even though we only found this yesterday. I should have
approached you yesterday.' He was sitting in front of
Simpson's desk. Simpson had a small office which was untidy, and cluttered. It offended Donoghue's sense of
orderliness. Donoghue took the photograph from the
envelope and handed it to Simpson. 'The samples you
first saw, Doctor Simpson, proved to be the work of a
hoaxer; everything you said about him proved to be correct. He went up before the Sheriff this morning.'

'Really?' Simpson looked up, he had a wide, puffy face.

'Yes, sir. He was young and immature like you indicated. He was remanded for three weeks for reports
before sentencing.'

'What will happen to him?'

'He'll probably get a few months in a Y.O.I.'

'Y.O.I.?'

'Young Offenders' Institution.'

'Ah.' Simpson bowed his head and looked at the
photograph. 'Well,' he said. 'This is more like it. You're
certain about the authorship of this?'

'Yes, sir. It was written by the killer.'

'Well, this was certainly written by someone who is
mentally disturbed.' He held the photograph sideways at
the desk so that Donoghue could see it. 'See how the
writing is bunched up, how it resembles a piece of string
that's tightly wound round itself, how tiny it is, how he's
used only a small area of the mirror surface, right at the
bottom. Notice also how the words are disjointed; letters
of the same words have a big gap between them and
in other parts letters of different words run into each
other.'

'What does it say about him?'

'It's an awfully small sample and I also can't help going
on what I've been reading in the papers, but I would say
he's a schizophrenic, the splitting of the words indicates

that, also, because of the smallness of the print, I'd say he was paranoid.'

'A paranoid schizophrenic.'

'Yes, acutely so. He's probably quite normal at his home or his place of work and then a change comes over him; something will be the trigger and then he goes out and kills. He probably thinks he's doing the right thing, acting in his victim's best interests. Psychopath is a lay term, it has no clinical meaning, but I would use it to describe the person who wrote this and is committing these murders. Off the record, of course.'

'Of course,' Donoghue nodded.

'Just looking at this writing makes me go cold,' said Simpson.

The second telephone call which upset Donoghue was the one which also annoyed him and it came at 5.45 that afternoon, shattering the one brief period of pleasure in Donoghue's day. He had read a communique from the Scottish Office in Edinburgh addressed to Chief Super-intendent Findlater. Findlater had written on it 'Handle this for me, will you, Fabian? — F.' The communique was notification that approval had been given for Frank Sussock's service to be extended. Donoghue looked for-ward to telling him. He had also just read Richard King's report on his arrest of Jamie McPherson and was not unimpressed. King had been a Detective-Constable for eighteen months and Donoghue pulled on his pipe, men-tally composing a memo to Findlater advising that King be promoted to Detective-Sergeant after completion of another six months' satisfactory service. He couldn't finish the memo, he was disturbed by his telephone ring-ing.

'Gentleman on the line for Mr Sussock, sir,' said the switchboard operator. 'I think he said his name's Alf Honso.'

'Alphonso,' said Donoghue, sitting forward and opening his notebook. 'Put him on, please.'

'Eh, Raymond,' said the voice, 'Sammy here, I've got something for you, Raymond. I've got the killer.'

'Who is it?' asked Donoghue excitedly.

'Eh, wait a minute. Who is *that*?'

'Inspector Donoghue, Mr Alphonse.'

'Where's Ray?'

'He's ill. I can take the information.'

'No. I talk only with Ray.'

'Mr Alphonse, if you know anything about this killer you must tell me.' Donoghue gripped the receiver but tried not to sound agitated. He didn't think he was being wholly successful. 'You are obliged by law to inform the police if you have knowledge of this sort and you can get into serious trouble if you withhold information.'

'Who's withholding information? I'm telling Ray.'

'I think you'd better tell me. What do you know about this man?'

'I know everything. I know who he is, I know where he lives, I know I'm right. I seen him, he looks the part, he sticks them in the stomach first.'

'Mr Alphonse . . .'

'Alphonso.'

'Mr Alphonso, I give you solemn warning that if you don't tell me, I shall prosecute you, I'll throw the lousy book at you, Alphonso.'

'O.K., so throw. I still only tell Ray.' Then he hung up.

Donoghue telephoned Ray Sussock's home. His wife answered. Donoghue asked for Ray. 'He's not here,' said Mrs Sussock in a thin, high-pitched voice. 'He's not been in for weeks. He's out catching robbers.' She hung up. Donoghue pressed the button for the desk sergeant on his internal phone.

'Sergeant Dover,' said the voice, calm, relaxed.

'Donoghue. I want Constable Willems in my office now.'

'She's off-duty, sir. She went off an hour ago.'

'Christ. Send a man to my room.' He banged the receiver down and scribbled a note on his memo pad: 'Head-banger. Tell Ray to contact Alphonso a.s.a.p. Also to contact me a.s.a.p. Donoghue.' He tore off the memo and pushed it into an envelope, and was sealing it as a young constable knocked and entered his office.

'Do you know where W.P.C. Willems lives?'

'I can find out sir, Sergeant Dover keeps . . .'

'Yes. Find out, then go there and give her that. If she's not in push it through her letterbox. It's an emergency. Off you go.'

Elka Willems had accepted a lift to the South Side. She had washed and changed and packed an overnight bag and walked back out to catch a northbound bus. Ray Sussock had that day taken a flat in the West End and she was going to spend the night there. She sheltered in a shop doorway on Pollockshaws Road, waiting for a bus. She saw a police car with a blue flashing light speed south. She thought nothing of it.

She took a No. 56 to George Street and crossed into George Square, head down against the snow. At Queen Street Station she stopped for a coffee in the buffet and looked out on to the forecourt of the station, where a young man with a ginger beard was sifting through the rubbish bins and a policeman was moving along a drunk. People stood waiting for trains. They looked wet and cold. Elka Willems drained her cup and, fortified, took a No. 16 bus to the bottom of Byres Road. She walked up Byres Road close against the buildings for shelter.

Ray Sussock opened the door at her second ring. He was dressed in pyjamas and dressing-gown. Elka Willems stepped inside quickly and took his arm.

'Poor Ray,' she said.

In the bedroom Sussock slipped off his dressing-gown and climbed back into his bed. Elka Willems poured a stiff shot of whisky, added some lemon and honey and topped it up with boiling water. She handed it to him. 'Drink up,' she said. 'It'll blow your head off.' She looked around her; the room was small, the furniture was old but warm-looking and solid. 'Cosy' was the word which occurred to her, as she took it in with a sweep of her eyes. 'Not bad, Ray, not bad, old Sussock. How much do you pay?'

'Fifty a month plus gas and electric.' He sipped at his toddy.

'Knock it off, Ray, don't sip at it.'

'It's hot.'

'Just drink it.' She began to peel her clothes off. 'Did you see your solicitor today?'

'I went this afternoon, just after I picked up the keys for this place. I should have stayed in, I only made my cold worse. I'll go in tomorrow, though. Anyway, I told him the situation, and he said that we should separate and raise an action for division and sale, which could take years.'

'So it takes years. Don't you feel better now that you're free of the bitch?'

Sussock sniffed. 'Anyway,' he said, braving the hot water and taking the toddy down in mouthfuls. 'About the house. I have to continue the mortgage payments until the separation papers come through, which only takes a matter of weeks, then I have to instruct him to raise this action for division and sale in the Sheriff Court, that could take years before it's finalized. In the meantime the Building Society will freeze the asset. When the hearing's over we sell the house, which she won't like, but the mortgage is in my name, we sell the house and pay off what we owe the Building Society and divide the residue. My solicitor is always on about raising actions.' He put the empty glass on the floor.

She unhooked her brassiere and stepped out of her panties. 'Mmm, will you be raising any action tonight, I wonder?'

Sussock grinned, 'Tell me the news from the office, worthy one.' He looked at her, blonde-haired, firm-breasted, wide-hipped.

'The big news from the station is that the ageing Detective-Sergeant Sussock has had his request for extended service approved.' She wriggled under the sheet and lay beside him. 'Where are you? . . . ah, there, nice and hard, goody.'

'How did you find that out?' He lay on his side, enfolding her in his arms, pulling her breasts against him.

'One of the cadets told me. He doesn't know about us, he just mentioned it in passing, over coffee.'

'One of the cadets! Is nothing sacred?'

'One of the secretaries told him. They read all the memos, the secretaries, especially the ones marked confidential, and they spill the beans to the cadets. They try to get off with the cadets, you see, because they all want to marry a policeman with a truncheon.' She began to unfasten his pyjamas. 'Now listen, old Sussock, I know that you are an ageing and tired and sick policeman, but this calls for a celebration, lie over on your back, good; now straighten your legs, that's it; now I'm going to make love to you and you are not allowed to move, not one muscle, not one inch . . . now, like so . . .'

Sussock groaned.

Three miles away, at the Social Work Department Offices in Parliamentary Road, the killer was murdering his social worker.

CHAPTER 11

Sadie McCafferty sat on a chair in the corridor, sobbing into a red handkerchief. A policewoman tried to comfort her. A policeman stood in front of a closed door. There was another policeman outside the building. Malcolm Montgomerie tried to work the strange switchboard, listening to clicks and buzzing and Mrs McCafferty before he finally heard the soft purr of an outside line. He dialled an Edinburgh number. It was 7.40 a.m., the 27th of January.

'Montgomerie here, sir, he's struck again.'

'Where?' Donoghue wiped the shaving lather from his chin and indicated to his wife to get his car from the garage. She ran from the room.

'Social Work Offices, Parliamentary Road.'

'When?'

'Last night. The cleaner discovered the body this morning when she arrived for work, the body's that of a social worker, the cleaner remembers this lady working late last night, she thinks she was interviewing someone.'

'What have you done?'

'Secured the building.'

'Is that all!'

'We've just got here, sir, I thought the first call should be to yourself.'

'Very well. Get the photographers and Forensic down, call the station and leave word for Ray Sussock to come over if he comes in and then call King at his home and have him come over to give you a hand.'

'I don't need King's help.'

'We both need all the help we can get, Montgomerie. Just get him there. I'll be with you in an hour.'

Montgomerie pulled the jack-plug out of the switchboard. 'See that guy,' he said loudly, but to nobody in particular. He replaced the jack-plug and called Forensic and the police photographers, and then Richard King.

King was the first of the three to arrive, he was there less than half an hour after receiving Montgomerie's call. Montgomerie showed him the corpse; it was the body of a middle-aged female dressed in tweeds with an expensive hairdo. She had a good bone structure and was a handsome woman who, in her youth, both police officers thought, would have been something of a beauty. She was lying at the side of her desk in a pool of blood. She had been stabbed in the stomach and neck and had sustained a deep gash down her left cheek. On the blotting-pad on her desk was written 'This is for Lissu'. It had been written in a felt-tip and the ink had feathered into the blotting paper, making the tiny scrawl barely legible. The filing cabinet in the room was four-doored dove-grey metal. It was unlocked and all files had been removed, leaving only a pair of soft indoor shoes, a jar of coffee, two tins of beans and a half-empty quarter-bottle of gin.

'Definitely the work of our friend,' said Montgomerie.

'No doubt about it,' King glanced at the open filing cabinet. 'You say she was seen talking with someone last night?'

'Not exactly. Her door was shut and the cleaner, Mrs McCafferty, heard her talking with someone. She was still talking at 6 p.m. when Mrs McCafferty left the building.'

'She didn't see this person arrive?'

'No such luck. Mrs McCafferty got here just at the back of five and she heard this lady talking with someone. They were still talking when she left. She came in this morning and found the body and made a three nines call.'

'That explains the ambulance outside.'

'Aye, she called them, but we got automatic notification and one of our cars got here first.'

'I wonder,' said King. 'I wonder. Have you called Fabian, Mal?'

'Aye. What do you wonder?'

'Well, let's toss this about with you. If the person was talking to this lady; what's her name?'

'Mrs Sommer.'

'O.K. If the person whom Mrs Sommer was talking to

late yesterday afternoon was known to her, I mean previously known to her, then he was known in one of two capacities, personal or professional. Right?'

'Right.'

'So if she was engaged in professional work then she had some information on this guy.'

'Right, the empty filing cabinet, he took his file.'

'And all the others to hide his ID.'

'There must be some sort of central index.'

'Wouldn't bank on it, Mal, these Welfare types wouldn't know efficient administration if it got up and smacked them in the jaw. What time do the staff come on duty?'

'Dunno. Start drifting in at around eight-thirty, I reckon. What does her diary say?'

'That's a good idea,' said King, and turned towards the desk. The page of the previous day had been torn from the diary. King knelt and looked from a low angle across the page, there was a series of indentations. 'Lady used a ball-point,' he said. 'Obliging of her.' He searched the desk drawers for a fine pencil, and, finding one, began to draw the point lightly across the page, skimming over the indentations. Holding the page open against the light from the table lamp he made out Mrs Sommer's diary entries on the day she died.

a.m. — duty
12.00 — hairdresser   Write up Maxwell file
2.00 — Mrs Kennedy   write Young report
5.30 — B.   close Donison

'I think it's a reasonable assumption, Watson,' said King, 'That our friend has a name beginning with B.'

Montgomerie said, 'By Jove, Holmes.'

There was a knock at the door. The constable who had been standing outside the room opened the door and said, 'Forensic and photography here, sir.'

King and Montgomerie left the room. Bothwell was in

the corridor, he looked tired and confused. Behind him there were two men carrying photographic equipment.

'Check the diary and the filing cabinet for fingerprints,' said King. 'We know they've been touched.'

'Fine,' said Bothwell.

'Any people outside?'

'A few, and Mr Donoghue's just arriving. He was parking his car as we came in.'

Donoghue entered the building, went straight to Mrs Sommer's office, and then joined King and Montgomerie in the main office of the building, where the switchboard was, where the desks and typewriters stood, where the walls were lined with banks of filing cabinets, and there was an IN/OUT board and a blackboard with 'J.P. not back—26/1' chalked on it. King told Donoghue what he and Montgomerie had found in Mrs Sommer's office.

'So we need someone to show us around this maze,' said Donoghue, putting his pipe in his mouth. 'Constable!'

The officer walked into the room from the corridor. He stood reverently with his hands clasped behind his back.

'There are some people outside, Constable,' Donoghue said to him. 'Most work here. Please find out if anyone works in the administrative section of this office, and if so ask them to come in.'

The constable said, 'Yes, sir,' and threw an unnecessarily smart salute and left the room. Donoghue took his coat off, King and Montgomerie followed suit. King noticed a poster on the wall; it showed a group of office workers falling about, and it had the caption 'You want it by when?!' King smiled and caught Montgomerie's eye and nodded towards the poster. Montgomerie laughed. Donoghue turned and saw the poster. He allowed himself a barely suppressed smile.

'Wonder if we could take a quick photocopy?' suggested Montgomerie.

'Wouldn't recommend you to,' said Donoghue drily.

The constable returned. Behind him was a young girl with glasses, who carried herself with a poor posture. 'Miss McGarvey, sir,' said the constable, and withdrew into the corridor.

'Thank you,' said Donoghue, lighting his pipe. 'Miss McGarvey, do you know what's happened here?'

'No. No, sir,' she was trembling slightly. 'Is it something to do with Mrs McCafferty, we saw her crying when they drove her away in a police car?'

'No. It's something to do with Mrs Sommer. I'm afraid she's dead.'

The girl looked unsteady. Donoghue yelled, 'Chair!' Montgomerie grabbed a chair and placed it behind the girl, who sank into it. She said, 'Dead?'

'Yes I'm afraid so. All her case files seem to have been taken away. I presume she did keep her case records in the filing cabinet in her room?'

'Yes, sir.' The girl looked very pale.

'We need to know the names and addresses of the people she was working with. Can you help us?'

'Let me see.' Her voice was still shaky. 'Yes, it'll be in Mr Harley's room. He keeps a list, just names; if I can get Mrs Sommer's list I can get the addresses from the central card index.'

'How long will that take?'

'Once I have the names, fifteen minutes, a bit longer.' She got up from the chair and left the room, still unsteady on her feet.

There were footsteps in the corridor. The constable said, 'Good morning, sir,' and Ray Sussock bustled into the room, holding a handkerchief against a streaming nose. He said, 'I heard the flap, so I came round.'

'Well, just get back, Sussock.' Donoghue turned on him with a venom neither King nor Montgomerie had seen before. 'Your bloody grass phoned in last night, said he knew the address of the killer, name too, but wouldn't give it, would only talk to you. Find him, get the information and then arrest him.'

'Arrest him!'

'Withholding information. If he had told me we might have prevented this.'

'What time did he phone?'

'Five thirty, five forty-five. It doesn't make any difference, I'll prosecute him for everything I can.'

'What time was the murder committed?'

'Some time after six,' said King, hoping to defuse the situation. 'But the murderer was already here by five o'clock.' Donoghue glanced at King.

'Wouldn't have made any difference, then,' said Sussock. 'By the time Sam Alphonso phoned in he was already here.'

'But he hadn't killed her, Ray, we might have got here in time.'

'We'll never know. I'll find him, but I'm not arresting him.'

'That's an order, Ray.'

'I'm disobeying it, sir.'

'Ray!'

'You'll look foolish in court. You'll never make the charge stick. He wasn't withholding information, he was selective about who he told.'

'You don't know what you're saying. This will finish you, Sussock.'

'You're losing credibility, sir,' said Sussock flatly. Then he blew his nose.

Donoghue fell silent. Montgomerie and King looked at him. Sussock sniffed.

Miss McGarvey entered the room holding a piece of paper. She sensed the atmosphere and stopped in the doorway. Donoghue said, 'Just go and find him, Ray.' Sussock left the room. Donoghue turned to the girl, 'Well, Miss McGarvey, shall we get to work?' He smiled, but his pulse was racing.

Ray Sussock walked outside, pushed through the crowd and climbed into his car. He turned the key and gunned the engine. 'God in Heaven,' he said.

He drove through the city, making poor time in the traffic queues, and with the slush and snow keeping his speed down whenever he met a clear stretch of the road. He had the heater on full and was wearing a heavy woollen overcoat. He still shivered. Sussock drove to Maryhill and ran up a stair to a single end. On the wall by the door someone had scribbled WOPS OUT. Sussock hammered on the door. When there was no answer he hammered again and kicked it sharply. From inside he heard a woman wail. Then came a torrent of words which Sussock didn't understand but which were obviously abusive. The door opened and a woman stood in the doorway. She had dark skin and black hair, she was in her forties and very round. She ranted at Sussock.

'Sam?' said Sussock.

The woman tossed her head back and made a sharp sucking sound. Then she shut the door. Sussock knew that Sam Alphonso had phoned in and therefore that he wanted to talk. He also knew that Sam ruled his wife with a capital R. She wasn't disobeying him. He went back down the stair.

It was snowing hard. Lumps of slush floated in the gutter like icebergs. Sussock knew that Sam Alphonso knew this city like an ant knows its nest. There were a thousand places between Bearsden and Bailliesten where Sam Alphonso might be, merging with the scenery, antennae twitching. Sussock stepped into a deep puddle and felt the whole world was against him.

He sat in his car. It was a Wednesday. Wednesdays and Thursdays are Giro days, lots of punters with money to spend. Sam Alphonso would go where the groups gather. Sam Alphonso makes a bit on the side selling pornography. He's small-fry and makes pocket money. He works from El Greco's, interesting goings-on in the back room of El Greco's. The front room of El Greco's would be full of punters because it was Wednesday and the Giros had come with the morning post. Sussock drove to El Greco's.

The front room of El Greco's was steamy with drying raincoats. There were men sitting round some of the tables and women sitting round some of the others; round some of the tables both men and women were sitting. The tables had yellow formica tops. All the men had stubble on their chins and some of the women had bruises on their faces which they wore like medals. They were in El Greco's to drink pale tea and eat stale buns. Babies were screaming.

Sussock walked up to the counter. El Greco pulled a lever on the geyser and boiling water poured into the out-size teapot. His arms were brown and hairy, they had veins which ran down the outside and were as thick as telegraph poles. He had once left three Highland Light Infantry boys senseless on the floor of a cafe in Nicosia and felt confident enough to settle in Glasgow and brag about it. He eyed Sussock with deepset eyes under dark hairy eyebrows.

'Sam Alphonso,' said Sussock.

'Polis?'

Sussock nodded. El Greco shrugged his shoulders.

'He's in the back room, is he?'

'No. He's not in the back room. Nobody's in the back room.'

'I want to check it out.'

'No need for you to check nothing out, polis. Nobody's in the back room. I told you.'

'Listen, this isn't a raid, I need to talk to Sam Alphonso, and I don't mean in a week's time. Right now I don't care what's going on in the back room, but I can make it a raid if you want me to. Between the Vice Squad and the

Public Health Department we'd put you out of business tomorrow. So let's do it the easy way.'

El Greco snapped the lid on the teapot. 'O.K.' he said. He walked to the end of the counter and through some swinging beads. Sussock followed him.

'No need for you to come.' El Greco turned and barred his way.

'I'm coming anyway.'

'It's not a raid?'

'It's not a raid.'

El Greco led the way down a dark stairway, lit only by a single bulb. At the bottom of the stairs was a white painted door. El Greco tapped on the door, Sussock pushed past him and opened the door. A projector was flickering and on the screen two men were making love to a woman, one at either end. Sussock switched the light on. A group of men were sitting round the table. One man pulled his hat down over his face.

'You said it wasn't a raid,' said El Greco.

'It's not. I haven't seen a thing.'

'Ray!' Sam Alphonso was sitting next to the projector. He smiled at Sussock.

'A bit early in the day for this, isn't it, Sam?'

'You know this yin?' asked one of the men.

'He's an O.K. polis. Anytime's O.K. for me especially when you got a wifie like I got a wifie.'

'Let's have a chat outside, Sam. Sorry about ruining the show, boys.'

One or two men grunted. Sam Alphonso got out of his seat and followed Sussock outside. They sat in the car.

'You phoned in last night,' said Sussock. 'He struck last night, just after you phoned. It'll be on the lunchtime news.'

'Sure I phoned in.' Sam lit a cigarette.

'You should've talked to my governor. He's set to carry your head off for withholding information and I don't know if I can stop him.'

'So don't try. Anyway, who was holding information back? I had a contact with a policeman and he wasn't in so I rang off.'

'O.K., Sam, let's have it. What do you know?'

'Everything.'

'I'll have to owe it to you, Sam. I don't have any ready on me, but I'll see you all right.'

'Ray, there's no charge for this yin.' He waved the cigarette in the air. 'You know the Glasgow scene, Ray, what the papers call the underworld, well, you just wouldn't believe the wheels that have been turning for to catch the head-banger.'

'So spill.' Sussock was genuinely amazed. He'd heard of the police and the underworld acting towards the same end, but he'd never experienced it. But then, he'd never hunted a psychopath before.

'I told you the stiletto was the key. Stiletto's harder to get than a chieftain tank, only a couple of guys in Big G would deal with a stiletto. So I put the word out, said it was for to get the head-banger, Slow Tom we called him then. What did you do with the hoaxer, Raymond, string him by his balls? So one guy tells me two years ago he imports a stiletto from the Smoke to fulfil an order. Anyway, the guy never collects, so he's left with twelve inches of bad news. You with me, Ray?'

'All the way.'

'So he stashes it under a junk heap. Leaves it there. Anyway, a weirdo has a shop down by the Barrows, he sells mili something.'

'Militaria.'

'Right. Anyway, the mili thing is all Nazi daggers and stuff and spiked balls on the end of a length of chain, and stilettos. Now *he* is a head-banger. First I think he is *the* head-banger when I visit. He's a bruiser with greased-down black hair and I ask him if he'd co-operate with the

polis and tell me has he sold that stiletto yet? He says
which stiletto and kicks me out. I mean *kicks*. So I see this
guy I know and go back to the shop, only this time I don't
go by myself. Anyway, on the second visit the head-
banger with the black hair very suddenly remembers
which stiletto. He also remembers selling it. Not many
people in Big G would fit the description he gave.'

'So give it. C'mon, Sam, we're in a hurry.'

'Wait. This is for free so I'm telling the story. So again
the word is out. Yesterday he was seen in a bar and
followed home. I got his address and phoned in last night
for to give you the address and the name on the door.'

Sam Alphonso gave Sussock an address in G40. Sussock
scribbled it on his pad.

'Listen, Ray, you didn't see nothing in there, you said?'

'I didn't see nothing,' said Sussock firmly.

Sam Alphonso stepped out of the car and stood in the
snow. 'I hope you saw nothing, Ray. Because if you saw
something you'll lose a good grass.' He shut the car door
and walked back to El Greco's.

Sussock's arm shot forward as he snatched for the
radio.

Marjorie Sommer had recorded her casework in files, one
file for each person or family, and each file had a cor-
responding card in the central index. Anita McGarvey
took the cards out of the index and laid them on a table
top. There were 63. Printed on the cards were name and
address of the person concerned, plus some coding which
Donoghue did not understand.

'Anything with a B,' he said, and King and Montgomerie sifted through the cards. They extracted sixteen.
'What else could "B" mean?' asked Donoghue, pulling on
his pipe.

'William,' said King. He took two more cards from the
remaining forty-seven.

'So,' said Donoghue. 'Our man is recorded somewhere among these eighteen cards. Miss McGarvey, what do these codings mean?'

'Well, sir,' her voice had calmed. 'Part 3 is old people wanting into a home.'

Donoghue took away four cards from the eighteen.

'44-1A and 44-1B, they're children under supervision.'

Ten more cards were removed.

'Section 12, well, that means working with a family where there's children.'

'A family! There's only one name on the card.'

'Aye,' said the girl, surprised that a police officer could be so ignorant about the central card index coding. 'There's only one name on any of the cards, but even the 44-1s and the Part 3s will have a whole family behind them.'

'So the "B" may not be recorded in the card index at all?'

'No. Only the case files have all the family members recorded.'

'Which he took away with him.' Donoghue blew out a plume of smoke.

'Miss McGarvey,' said King. 'Do you know of anyone who'd murder Mrs Sommer?'

'A name with a "B"?'

'That would help.'

'Well, see, just before Christmas, Miss McCourt, that's another Social Worker, she had a breakdown. She was found doing the breaststroke down the corridor and when she reached the end she'd come back doing the back crawl. She was taken to Gartloch Hospital shortly after that. Anyway, the other workers shared her cases out, and Mrs Sommer took some. I haven't altered all the cards yet. There was this one guy, funny shifty eyes, used to be Miss McCourt's and went to Mrs Sommer. They never seemed to get on.'

'Name?'

'Bernard McWatt.'

'For God's sake!' yelled Donoghue.

'I'll get the card,' said Anita McGarvey.

'Excuse me, sir,' a constable stood in the doorway of the office; he held an open notebook. 'Radio message from Sergeant Sussock just came in, sir.'

'Well, what is it?' snapped Donoghue. 'Get on with it!' The constable read from his notebook. 'Message is, "Suspect's name believed to be McWatt, no Christian name, address believed to be 15 Dalmally Toll, G40".'

'Here it is, sir.' Anita McGarvey held up a small pink card.

'Address?'

'15 Dalmally Toll, sir.'

Dalmally Toll was a cul-de-sac of four-storey tenements. The red sandstone had turned dark brown and the paint was peeling. It had been built as a through road to the river, but an elevated four-lane expressway had caused the demolition of most of Dalmally Toll and forced cul-de-sac status on that which had been spared.

Sussock was waiting in his car outside the close mouth of No. 15. Donoghue pulled up behind him. Behind Donoghue was a car containing King and Montgomerie and behind them a patrol car with two constables inside and a revolving light on the roof. Curtains along both sides of Dalmally Toll were being drawn back even before the patrol car halted. It was snowing hard; the pavements and cobbled street lay under mounds of snow and banks of grey slush. Sussock blew his nose.

'You should be in bed, Ray,' said Donoghue.

'I'm not going to miss this, sir.'

'Been up there yet?'

'No.'

'Good. His address checks out with the card in the

Welfare Office. This is our man, Ray.'

'Alphonso is a good grass.'

'Aye,' said Donoghue drily. 'We'll be talking about that.' He turned to King and Montgomerie and the two constables. 'Nice thing about tenements, no rear entrances. We go in in force, let him make a play, but I don't think he'll need heavy handling. One constable to stay at the close mouth, the other with us.'

The door with 'McWatt' screwed to it was on the second floor of the stairway. They bunched round it; Donoghue took his ID from his jacket pocket and Sussock rapped on the door. The door of the opposite side of the landing opened and a middle-aged woman stood looking at the policemen. 'O.K., hen,' said the constable. The woman retreated, closed the door behind her and peered through the letterbox.

Sussock rapped on the door again. He could sense the tension rising in the group which stood around him.

He thought Sam Alphonso was a good grass, he thought he had a good argument, and he didn't want Donoghue to lose to him. In the basement he had seen something, he'd seen two men having a woman at once. And he'd seen a man holding his hat hard against his face. He knocked on the door again.

Donoghue turned to the constable. 'Go and see if he's shinning down the drainpipe.' The constable's boots clattered down the stair; halfway down he saved time by shouting to his mate: 'Jack! Drainpipe. Back court.'

Then the door opened with a gentle click. It swung wide; there was a woman standing in the darkness. She was bent and had silver whiskers on her chin and a red shawl draped over her shoulders. She leaned forward on an aluminium walking-frame.

'Mrs McWatt?' Donoghue showed her his ID. 'Is Bernard at home?'

'No.'

'Do you mind if we come in? We have some questions and we'd like to look around.'

'Yes, I mind,' said the woman. 'But I dare say you've got to.'

She turned slowly round and made her way into the gloom. The constable came running up the stair. He glanced at Donoghue and shook his head. The policemen followed the woman down the hall; the constable was the last in; he shut the door gently behind him and stood in front of it.

The woman slowly made her way to the living-room and stood in front of an electric fire. It was a cluttered room, there was an old television set in the corner, a canary in a cage by the window, a heavy settee and an old piano pushed up against the wall.

King wondered how they had got the piano up the stairs.

'Is Bernard in trouble?' The woman directed her question to Donoghue.

'He may be, Mrs McWatt. We'd like to talk to him.'

'Nobody can talk to him.'

'How no'?'

'Och, he's away with the fairies.'

'How's that?'

'Months now he's been sitting and brooding. He scares me. He spends a lot of time in his room. He brings books home and sits in his room reading them. Sometimes he sits in that chair there just looking at the bird and then he'll get up and go out. In this weather! Sometimes it's late when he goes out, after I'm in bed. I know he's been up and out because he's taken the cloth off the bird-cage.'

'Which is his room, Mrs McWatt?'

'Second along.'

'When did you last see him, Mrs McWatt?'

'This morning, when he left for work.'

'Where's that?'

'Cowcaddens. The Sheltered place.'

Donoghue turned round, but Montgomerie was already on his way.

The second room along the hall was a small room, some twelve feet by six feet, there was room for one bed, a wardrobe and a small desk on which stood a portable typewriter. Books lay on the floor, neatly stacked against the wall opposite the bed. King kneeled and looked at the books. There was little fiction, most were factual texts and most were historical. Donoghue entered the room. 'Look for something Oriental, Ancient Chinese. Go careful, don't disturb any evidence. This it *it*.' He returned to the sitting-room.

'What does Bernie do in his spare time?'

'Sits and reads. Sits and broods.'

'Social life?'

'None to speak of.'

'How old is he?'

'Thirty-seven. Do you know about Bernie, sir, what he's like? He's hardly ever had a social life, sometimes he goes into the bar across the street when it's quiet. He could never overcome his shyness.'

King brought a book into the room. It was a large hardback and he carried it delicately in gloved hands. He put it on the settee. 'Found it under the bed, sir.'

The book was called *Ancient Chinese Dynasties*. Donoghue opened the front cover; there was a small piece of notepaper, folded twice and tucked inside the dust-jacket. Donoghue took the paper, unfolded it and read it. It was written in the same disjointed, tightly screwed handwriting that he had shown to Mr Simpson of the Department of Applied Psychology. What was written was:

Order	Due	
male	16 Jan	on time

female	17 Jan	on time
female	18 Jan	on time
old female	21 Jan	one day late
the class female	24 Jan	on time
the Welfare lady	26 Jan	on time

It was the last entry which chilled Donoghue:
female   27 Jan
He turned to Mrs McWatt. 'What was he like this morning, before he left for work?'

'Quiet, sir. Kept looking at the floor.'

'What time was he in last night?'

'Late. About eight. He smelled of smoke.'

'He stayed in all night?'

'I don't know, sir. I go to my bed at eight-thirty. I don't see him again until the morning. He could have gone out again, but not in this weather, surely?'

'Was he up before you this morning?'

'Aye.'

'Was the cover off the bird-cage?'

'Aye.'

Donoghue began to pray that Bernie McWatt was at his work.

The man was slightly built, with a moustache, and was wearing a grey smock; his desk was Department of Employment standard issue; made of mild steel and painted in two tones of grey. There was a pipe running down the wall of his office. He stood as Montgomerie entered the room and vigorously shook his hand as though honoured by the policeman's presence. Montgomerie showed him his ID.

'It concerns Bernard McWatt, Mr Bonini. Is he at work?' Bonini sat down and picked up the phone on his desk. He indicated the chair in the front of his desk and Montgomerie sat down. 'Miss Watson, is Bernard

McWatt in today . . . yes, I'll hold . . . No? Thank you.'
He replaced the receiver. 'No, he hasn't clocked in. Quite
usual, I'm afraid, at least since Christmas.'

'Oh?'

'Well, since just before Christmas, really, funny how
Christmas is always a big milestone; but I digress, just
before Christmas he began to change, became moody,
not talking as much as he did, and has been absent a lot.
We tried to get in touch with his social worker, but she's
ill, apparently; pity, nice jovial lass with a woolly hat, she
was; anyway, he saw another worker, but I don't think
they get on too well. That's another pity because this is
the only job he can get and he's in danger of losing it.
This is the West of Scotland, you fight tooth and claw for
a job here and hold on to it for your life. Can I ask what
it's about?'

'I think you'll find out soon enough, Mr Bonini, but I
don't want to say anything right now. I wonder, could you
let me have a list of his absences and a sample of his handwriting?'

'Yes, yes, I dare say I can.' He reached for the
telephone.

'What does he do here?'

'He spray-paints metal chairs. Miss Watson, I wonder if
you could come in here for a moment, please.' He put the
phone down. 'Yes, he's been with us for about eight months,
he started in stores like all the others and then moved on
to painting. He was doing well and we were going to move
him on to fixing seats, but then his absences started. We
couldn't seem to talk to him; our own Welfare Officer,
Miss Hughes, gave him a lot of time but couldn't get
through and so she advised him to go and see his own
social worker. He's not the most alert person at the best of
times, if you see what I mean, but he seemed far away occasionally, usually he was his chirpy self, but he'd get
these moods. Moods don't mean anything, but he damaged

himself through his absences.'

Montgomerie walked away from the Sheltered Workshop holding a large manilla envelope in which was Miss Hughes's file on Bernard McWatt ('I'm not sure if this is at all correct, Mr Montgomerie . . .'), a sample of McWatt's handwriting and a list of his absences. He sat in the area car and shook his head. 'Not there,' he said, not looking at any of the three officers. 'Back to the station, please.'

Donoghue leaned against the wall; Montgomerie and Sussock sat at the table. Montgomerie held his head in his hands and Sussock was doodling on a piece of waste paper. The duty constable sat at the telephone. The windows were steaming up. King entered the room carrying a tray full of mugs of steaming tea. He put the tray on the table and kicked the door shut with his foot. Donoghue reached forward for his mug: there was a goat embossed on the white enamel. 'He's our man,' said Donoghue. 'According to that file he's spent years in Gartloch's secure ward, and he's on the town tonight with a knife. Comments.'

'We'll have to issue his description to all beat officers and patrol cars.' King stirred his tea.

'Saturate the city centre with officers, plain-clothed and uniformed,' Montgomerie suggested.

'So he strikes in High Possil,' snorted Sussock. 'Lot of good a hundred and fifty officers in George Square are going to do then, aye!'

'Cut it out!' Donoghue said sharply and then drank some tea before speaking again. 'Come on, there must be more suggestions. I know what I think we should do, but I want to hear your ideas.'

'Publicize it,' said Montgomerie. 'Name, description, and the fact he's on the town the night.'

'We'll find the bugger strung up from a lamp-post,' said Sussock.

'Aye,' agreed King. 'And a lot of broken heads as rival groups of punters fight for the trophy.'

'There'll also be an old lady in G40 with her door kicked in,' said Donoghue flatly. 'No, that won't do. I've seen mob violence before, I don't want to see it again.'

'O.K., O.K.' said Montgomerie, looking at the table. 'You asked for suggestions.'

'All right.' Donoghue swilled his tea round his mug. 'Let's look at his M.O. Brainstorm!'

'Night worker,' said Montgomerie, quickly.

'Right.'

'Mainly City Centre,' said King.

'Do you think you can say that?' asked Donoghue. 'Two out of six were attacked in the City Centre. We can't count Mrs Sommer because she was known to him and he would have gone to wherever her work place was, which just happened to be fairly central.'

'He's after a woman the night,' said Sussock. 'And he'll use a knife.'

There was silence in the room. Snow lay on the ledges outside the window.

'All right,' said Donoghue. 'What have we got? He's out on the town tonight, looking for a female to knife because his mother's bloody canary told him to do it. He's struck four times in the City Centre and the West End. It's only half an hour's walk from Buchanan Street to Byres Road so we'll look on that as our area. He's killed once in the South Side and he waited in her house for her to come home, that suggests he knew her or had seen her some place, probably in a magazine. Significance?'

'He won't be hunting a random target south of the river,' said Montgomerie.

'Right. All the people he has killed and has not previously known or seen have been attacked in the area I just outlined, West End to City Centre. That's his patch, his hunting ground. We ought to have noticed sooner.

But that's where he'll be tonight, because Li-Ssu, or the canary, didn't identify a particular target; his list just says "female". So we'll set a trap for him. Constable, is WPC Willems on duty?'

'Yes, sir.'

'Ask her to come up, please.'

Ray Sussock went very, very white.

Look at these books. I mean, look at them. There's a word, million, means a lot. There must be a million books in this library. I don't know why I haven't found it before. Books, books, books, and this is only one floor. Right here it's books about Africa. I could see this building when I learned the second one, the way she backed on to the building site like I had a mad dog in my hand, anyway, the big dome was against the sky. When I learned her I went to look at it. I just stood there looking at the dome with the stars in the background. I'll stay here. It shuts at eight. I'm a bit tired, burning all those files. Three trips, it took. Still, she knows now. I'm not going to work. When you're going to learn one you need rest, to prepare. Lissu wants me to learn one the night. I'll stay here till it shuts. Resting. Reading.

The woman was walking down the street. She was taller than most women, had long black hair, a dark leather coat, dark hat, and black boots. She walked purposefully, taking the snow in long but not inelegant strides. She looked like any young and attractive woman setting out late at night on the long walk home, except that in her shoulder-bag was a .38 Webley.

It was 3.45 a.m.

She had been walking since 10 p.m. Just walking. Her legs ached, five and three quarter hours is a long time for anyone to be walking. When it's five and a half hours through slush, and then a snowfall settles on the slush, which in the meantime had turned to ice, then it's an even longer time to walk.

The city was deserted, the fights had been fought, the drunks were in the cells, the injured in the casualty wards, the last buses had gone and the streets were quiet. The city was an area of captivating, awesome mysteriousness, but that didn't prevent her legs from getting sore. They were sore on the inside of her thighs, her feet ached and swelled inside her boots. She thought more about the ache in her legs than she did about the sensation in her stomach.

The sensation in her stomach was of hollowness and was caused by being intensely afraid. It was one thing using plain clothes for surveillance, but it was something else again to use plain clothes to act as bait for a deranged killer. Throughout the night she rarely walked more than two hundred yards without once thinking that there was more than one punter on the town that night who was away with the fairies. In the snow in front of her were four sets of footprints made by a woman wearing a size 6 boot or shoe with a wide 'sensible' heel. At the side of the woman's prints were four sets of prints made by a man wearing large, flat-heeled shoes. Four times up Buchanan Street since the snow stopped, and Donoghue snug and warm in his Rover, just out of sight, passing round the flask of coffee and a nip of brandy. Och, you're off your head, Willems. She carried on walking only because the man following her would catch her up if she stopped.

Donoghue had parked his car in the gloom of an alley near Queen Street Station. He hadn't a coffee flask or nip of brandy to pass around, nor did he have any company. He was alone with his thoughts and his thoughts plagued him that he was wrong, that it wasn't going to work, that he wasn't just making a blunder, he was making a *blunder*. He also knew that by not telling Findlater of the operation he was laying his whole career on the line. There was a song going through his head. That morning as he was driving to Glasgow with the radio on he had switched from Radio Four as *Thought for the Day* started and got a music station and had heard a song called *The Gambler*. A line in the song had stuck in his mind; 'You've got to know when to fold them.' Donoghue thought he hadn't known when to fold his deck, he thought he'd played all his cards and hadn't a penny in the bank and he'd mortgaged his soul to stay in the game.

The operation was a big one. He had issued orders above his station and had had the West End saturated with uniforms and cars after midnight. Not so much to catch the killer but to force him into the quieter City Centre around which a tight net had been discreetly slung. He knew it was a long shot and by 3.30 he knew it wasn't going to work. His thoughts were torturing him and he had relief only once every half-hour, when Elka Willems would pass the end of the alley in which he was parked and when he would pick up the walkie-talkie which lay beside him and say 'Point Fifteen. Dog sighted.' Forty seconds later, when the lanky form of PC Hamilton also passed the end of the alley, he would speak again into the mouthpiece of the walkie-talkie, 'Point Fifteen. Fox sighted.'

Elka Willems turned from Argyle Street and into Buchanan Street for the fifth time since the snow had stopped falling. Her legs were very sore. She was feeling very tired; she no longer bothered that this was one of the parts of the route which worried her the most: when she rounded the corner she would be out of sight of Phil Hamilton for twenty seconds. She was too tired to care any longer. Buchanan Street was quiet, with a shroud of snow lying evenly over the pedestrian precinct.

When the stiletto plunged into her stomach she was so tired that her first reaction was to look down at the man who was killing her and grin at the absurdity of it all. Then she went cold, a chill shot down her spine. The knife was pulled out of her, she fell forwards and saw the knife coming upwards. She deflected it and fell to the ground, grabbing the arm holding the knife, a small, strong arm, which continued to pull and lunge for her throat. The man had a fierce Viking face, brilliant ginger hair and beard, he danced round her, snorting like a pig, trying to pull his arm free. She wanted to say 'police' but there was blood in her mouth. Finally she screamed.

Phil Hamilton's heart seemed to explode when he heard the scream. He grabbed his radio and said, 'Control. Fox. Contact. Contact. Buchanan Street, Argyle Street. Assistance required.' Then he ran, ran with clumsy ungainly steps slipping outwards in the snow. The night was suddenly pierced by two-tone klaxons, and Hamilton saw a blue flashing light racing through Anderston Cross towards him. He slid round the corner and into Buchanan Street, he said, 'Christ' and then yelled, 'Police!'

He saw the figure kick away from Elka Willems, who sagged to the ground. The figure ran across the snow in a curious leaping gait, it was small and round, black against the whiteness. Hamilton chased the man, running past the groaning policewoman. He heard a car turn into Buchanan Street and follow him. Hamilton didn't turn: he knew instinctively that it was Ray Sussock.

The figure ran to the sculpture and Hamilton lost sight of it momentarily among the benches and evergreens and waste-bins. He stopped and pulled his truncheon from his pocket. The car behind him stopped, Sussock got out and stood beside him. Two patrol cars, lights flashing, drove down Buchanan Street abreast. Halfway down they stopped and four policemen got out of each car and stood in a row across the street, in front of the cars. Behind the cars Hamilton noticed a green Rover slow to a halt. He smiled.

Lowly as he felt himself to be, he was glad Donoghue was going to be in at the finish.

Hamilton and Sussock walked towards the shrubs. Behind them a transit van pulled up. Police officers jumped out; two ran to where Elka Willems lay and six and a sergeant formed up behind Sussock and Hamilton.

The figure broke from the bushes and ran diagonally across Buchanan Street. Hamilton ran after him; behind him he could hear the panting breaths and the heavy footfalls of eight men running. The officers at the top of the street ran down towards the figure.

The figure turned and stopped. He looked up and down the street and laughed. The laugh echoed off the buildings and stopped the policemen in their tracks. For three seconds, perhaps five, the figure held the police at bay, just by standing in the snow laughing, and holding a bloody knife above his head.

Sussock pulled the .38 from his coat pocket.

The figure turned and ran into the alley. Hamilton held up his hand. 'That's a blind alley', he announced. 'No way out.' Hamilton and Sussock walked to the entrance of the alley. They were joined by the officers who ran from the top of the street. Three policemen stood in a line, Sussock, Hamilton, and another constable Hamilton recognized as Piper, the confident Constable Piper, who had walked with him to the top of a derelict tenement and who had shone his torch unflinchingly on what they had found there.

In the alley the quarry turned to face the hounds. He stood and laughed his icy laugh, which Sussock knew would stay with him for the rest of his life, another noise to haunt him in the small hours. Hamilton wondered if he laughed like that at his victims? Was that laugh the last thing they heard before he reached down and cut their throats? The man threw the stiletto; it flew wildly through the air and bounced off Piper's tunic. He laughed again, drew another knife from the pocket of his donkey jacket and in the same movement pulled the blade across his throat. His breast flushed red and he collapsed in the snow.

The three men looked down at the figure lying in the snow. It was barely four feet long.

Donoghue put the phone down and sat behind his desk. He smiled at Ray Sussock who sat opposite him. 'She's going to be all right, Ray,' he said, and reached for his pipe.

'Thank God,' sighed Sussock.

'Aye.' Donoghue put his pipe in his mouth. 'She was nearly No. 7, and I was nearly a traffic warden. I still may be. Anyway, the raid on El Greco's is fixed for seven tomorrow morning. It was heavy, sadistic stuff, you say?'

'Yes,' said Sussock. 'If that was a sample it was as heavy as we've ever had.'

'O.K. We have the building under surveillance, so they can't shift it without us knowing. I've talked to Prosecution about Alphonso and they reckon we've got a case, if you'll tell us where we can collar him.'

'He has a single end in Maryhill. But you never know where he's likely to be.'

'Give the address to Montgomerie, he can bring him in this afternoon.'

'I still think you're fighting a difficult case that will be embarrassing to lose. And I'm losing a good grass.'

'The case will be open and shut. He'll likely get three years. Look, Ray, he phoned in with the information at a quarter to six on the night McWatt killed his welfare officer. If he had given me the information, how long would it have taken for us to get to his mother's house?'

'Fifteen minutes.'

'Less. Then we find the list inside that book; he wrote his orders down before he fulfilled them, so we would know where he was; there's only one welfare office he could be in, they operate a patch system in this city. By this time it's a few minutes after six so we radio the nearest mobile to get there fast. We know the welfare officer was alive at six, because that's when the cleaner left. We might have made it in time, Ray, but we'll never know, Alphonso didn't give us or Mrs Sommer a chance to find out, because he thought he was important. He's going to do time.'

Sussock was silent. Then he said, 'But he found the head-banger, sir.'

'I don't think he did. I think the underworld found him. They sent Alphonso on errands and gave him support when he needed it and they accepted him as mediator. If you're still upset about it, look upon it as protective custody, because when it gets around what a mess he made of the transfer of information, then,' Donoghue waved his palm, 'if he wasn't inside he'd be at the bottom of the Clyde.'

'O.K.,' said Sussock. 'I won't argue any more. Now it's the more difficult call, I suppose?'

'Aye.' Donoghue sucked his pipe. 'How do you think he'll take it?'

'I think he'll flap like a turkey that's just found out about Christmas. What are you going to say?'

'Tell the truth, the whole truth and nothing but. What else can a policeman say?'

'Some would argue that one. You'll be disciplined. You'll lose rank.'

'Probably.'

'Would you like me to go?'

'Not unless you want to, Ray. I won't be implicating you in any way. The buck stops here.'

'I'd like to stay.'

'As you wish.' Donoghue reached for the telephone, turning as he did so, and glanced out of the window. It was ten after nine, and the dawn was an awe-inspiring crimson cloudbank, streaked with black bands. Donoghue knew then why primitive people worshipped the sun. The line clicked, and he said, 'Chief Inspector Findlater, please.'